AN2   9.5v

D0245967

The
Beekeeper

The Beekeeper

KEITH HENDERSON

Illustrated by

NORMAND COUSINEAU

DC Books   Montreal   1990

Cover design and typography by Zibra, Inc.

Illustrations and cover painting by Normand Cousineau.

Typeset in Times by DCAD Enterprises, Montreal.

Printed and bound in Canada by Les Editions Marquis Ltée.

Special editing by Mireille Bertrand and Suzanne Charron.

Dépot légal, Bibliothèque nationale du Québec
and the National Library of Canada, 3rd trimester, 1990.

The publishers acknowledge the assistance of the Canada Council.

Canadian Cataloguing in Publication Data

Henderson, Keith, 1945-.
The Beekeeper.
ISBN 0-919688-22-5   (bound).--
ISBN 0-919688-21-7   (pbk.).

I. Title

PS8565.E55B44   C813'.54   C90-090337-6
PR9199.3.H46B44   1990

DC Books, 1495 rue de l'Eglise, Box 662, Montreal, PQ, H4L 4V9

"...Stung with the maddening trance of Dionysus."

— Euripides

i

LIKE MANY YOUNG MEN of twenty in those later years of the 1960's, Walter Taylor wanted to leave home but had discovered too many reasons why he couldn't. Really there were only two, university courses and Helen Morris, a low-slung, pudgy girl Walter found quite delicious in the heavy, creamy sort of way he'd decided he liked best. For his education Walter bore little allegiance. For Helen he bore little more, except that he had yet to sleep with her, or anybody else he was ashamed to say, and considered her the likeliest means to dispose of the problem. However, the prospect of doing this alternately terrified him or left him with a vague feeling of discontent, particularly when a friend, in his most indulgent manner, began prescribing things for him, like the novels of D.H.

Lawrence. For the longest time Helen would simply squirm away whenever he tried to do anything too deliberate, like unzipping her shorts. This would first frighten, then annoy him. They would spend the rest of the evening watching television or drinking instant coffee.

Both these problems were solved, however, as such problems often are, the first by a stout French professor by the name of Madame de Bissonet. A fellow student once told Walter she had a penchant for female students, whom she would regularly invite up to her apartment to make dressings for African lepers. After this he began to suspect the worst. What other explanation was there for her disdain for young men? Why else would she sit them at the front of the class where she could torment them with preposterous questions?

On one particular morning Walter determined to make an issue of this. He moved to the back. At first he'd thought better of it, but he quickly convinced himself that his rights were at stake. Surely he was old enough to decide where he would sit!—though he soon realized the extent of his error. Madame looked up from her attendance sheets and fixed him with a gaze of splendid Parisian horror. He moved. Madame de Bissonet pointed to the front, then paused as her injured dignity limped about the room. Calmly, unprotestingly, Walter Taylor moved.

"Mais vite, monsieur Taylor! Vite! On n'a pas toute la journée!"

He did resolve never to return, however, despite the fact that it was mid–January and attendance was compulsory. When he didn't pass the year, Walter considered it a great moral victory.

[10]

During the early summer, things had gone rather badly with Helen Morris too. Her father was now disturbed that his daughter was seeing a young man who worked as a labourer on the highways, a fact which pleased Walter enormously. He took to wearing his workpants over to their house. In the face of her father's objections, Helen's affections were tentative enough, but she did manage to get him to suffer Walter's invitation to their country home—mostly, Walter reminded her, because he thought he'd have somebody to help him put an extension on his garage. Her father hadn't reckoned on Walter's general ineptitude with tools. Nevertheless, in the idyllic surroundings of a late June weekend, and on an entirely different plane, Walter Taylor had finally been successful, if that was the term.

All that Saturday afternoon Mr. Morris had kept Walter working on his garage. But on the Sunday Walter managed to slip away with Helen in her father's canoe. They paddled up a short, sluggish river that connected two small lakes in the region, keeping abreast of the shore to avoid the powerboats that used the river more or less as a canal. To Walter, these powerboats simply contained assorted versions of Helen's father, middle-aged Ontario men in shorts whom he learned to despise as complacent and bourgeois. He disliked them even more for disturbing his sense of decorum: the black water, the low overhanging willows, and Helen's attractive body moving languidly at the front of the canoe, all of which he had fashioned into a scene worthy of the Renoir prints he had just bought. The comparison delighted him, and when two or three more powerboats passed them by, sending their

"...the black water, the low overhanging willows..."

wakes slapping and skittering to the side and nearly upsetting the canoe, Walter pursed his lips in contempt and put ashore at the first suitable landing.

"These businessmen," he said.

Helen looked at him blankly.

They had landed at a flat, muddy little place with an unoccupied summerhouse overlooking the bank. Walter was in a particularly anxious mood. He had had enough (or so he told himself), and he grasped Helen by the hand a little roughly as he helped her up the bank. His mind was made up. He led her to an old picnic table at the front of the house where he sat down deliberately and made love to her. He let his hand wander authoritatively about in the bottom part of her black new swim–suit until the lower reaches of her body had collapsed to the state of a mushy pudding. Walter was amazed at the speed with which this happened. "No more than thirty seconds!" he said to himself with some pride. Occasionally he would bite her chin, and when finally the planks of the seed–strewn table began to get a little uncomfortable, he jumped down, adjusted his swimming trunks, and led her across a tiny mud–creek into a neighbouring pasture.

"Where are we going?" she asked.

"For a walk," Walter answered.

But this didn't satisfy her.

"Where are we going?" she persisted, this time with a slightly frantic tone to her voice.

"Just over here," Walter said as he pulled her down in the grass.

"Not my pants," she said as Walter reached for the elastic top and slid them down.

But Walter paid no attention. He was engrossed. She *was* the best thing he had ever seen, and for a moment he just gazed at her.

"That will never fit into me," Helen finally said looking down at him.

"Oh, yes it will. It's made for that," said Walter gallantly, and with that he tried to enter her, at first gently and then when she wouldn't budge, with an increasing insistence that bordered on consternation. But she was stuck fast. Try as he may, he couldn't get into her, and when the big blue–backed pasture flies began to settle on her, no doubt attracted by the scent, Helen began to cry, partly from pain and mostly from humiliation.

"What's the matter?"

"I want to go home," Helen sobbed. "I want to go home *now*."

Walter leaned over to kiss her, but Helen rushed to her feet. "Where are my pants?" she yelled.

Walter looked at her quizzically.

"Where are my pants!"

"How the hell do I know!" Walter said rolling over decisively on his stomach.

"You're lying on them. Will you give me my pants please?"

Walter wouldn't look at her. He reached under his leg and held the pants over his back. Helen took them and put them on.

"Are you coming?"

Walter snapped around, grabbed his trunks, and put them on in one motion, secretly pleased they hadn't caught and forced him to curse and tussle. He followed Helen back to the canoe. Two weeks later she told him she was moving to London, Ontario to live with her aunt.

For a week after Helen's phone call, Walter went down to sit in his basement room and smoke. He liked to smoke whenever he was disgusted. He particularly liked to smoke in his basement room—an ordered, backward looking little place, filled with a distant afternoon sunshine angling sharply in from two high windows that peeped over his mother's rambling attempt at an English country garden. Walter had filled it with furniture rescued from his grandfather's shed, relics too outdated even for his maiden aunts who were nevertheless glad he'd taken an interest in them. Years in an unheated shed had splayed the legs and cracked the veneer on many pieces; on others the stain had blistered and granulated, but Walter took them away and arranged Renoir prints over them, smooth–assed, buttery young women, like young heifers, but curiously over–ripe. Underneath this vision of perfection, Walter pondered the problem of Helen Morris.

She was buttery enough, it was true, and her plump milkmaid figure did ample justice to the nudes in his Renoir prints, but she was also dull, with the special dullness of expensive middle–class fakery, vinylized wood panelling, electric fireplaces, the tastelessness of which Walter now deprecated whenever he got the chance. He would draw Helen's attention to the oak beams fitted into the stucco at the front of her house and scoffed at the name of her subdivision—Tudor Manor Estates. He championed disciplined taste and studiously abhorred sentimentality.

He also hated her cat, with a strenuous, passionate hatred. Helen spent much of her time fussing with this, a skinny rat–like animal called Jessica which she would regularly dandle in her arms and kiss while it kicked and struggled to get down. Once when she had squirmed away from him only to fling little Jessica over her shoulder and whisper some baby–talk into its ear, Walter had frowned, folded his arms, and lapsed into one of his most menacing silences.

"What do you have to kiss the thing for?" he finally asked. "You're not its mother."

"It's not it. It's a she!" Helen had retorted tearfully and run upstairs.

Jessica's origins had been the occasion for some even more lofty contempt. In October of the previous year, Mrs. Morris had arranged for a friend's prize blue–point Siamese to mate with their tabby as part of Helen's little brother's sex education. This was all to take place in the basement. The lights were dimmed while he, the family, and a select group of neighbours had sat around in lawn chairs waiting for the male to be released from a large wicker basket. The moment arrived. But after a few exploratory cuffs and a great deal of howling, there followed so much spitting and vicious carrying on that little Robert had to be taken from the room in tears. Even Mrs. Morris had misgivings and asked for the whole thing to stop, but her husband, who had looked on with clinical severity, wouldn't hear of it. As for Helen, she became reconciled with the whole process only when it produced little Jessica.

"Sentimentality," Walter Taylor remarked to himself, as he spat out a painfully bitter drop of juice from the pipe he'd taken up the year before because he felt it added to his sense of weight and personal presence. He'd given himself over to contempt, contempt for her father, contempt for her father's job and his political convictions, contempt for her mother and her varicose veins (which he felt sure Helen would inherit), contempt for the life he had been leading. What had he done after all? What had he seen? Hadn't he read that life was to be lived like a work of art? And here he was, always frayed and disconsolate, forever surrounded by tedium and banality. More and more the solution appeared to him. Leave. Have done with his petty tormentors—preferably with as little explanation as possible. Disappear on them. For a moment the thought of never seeing Helen again crossed his mind. Then he snorted.

"What can she do?" he asked himself. "What can she think? She can't draw. She can hardly read. All she can do is fuss with that idiot cat."

ii

LOSING HIS JOB on the roads had been a chastening experience too, to say the least. Walter had come by the work easily enough, just walked up to the construction shack and asked the Polish foreman if they needed any more men. They did. Walter got a hard hat and a pneumatic drill, which he'd never used before in his life; then he and Lennie Cuppola, who'd done the same thing a week earlier, found themselves breaking up concrete on a twenty foot tall collector sewer. In theory they were supposed to stand on the lip and drill chunks off into the hole. Simple enough, except the weight of the drill would almost pitch Walter into the hole every time the bit tore through the concrete. Then there were the iron rod re–enforcement bars. What in hell did you do with iron rod re–enforcement bars? Lennie didn't know. At break, they would discuss strategies, listen to Hans Mueller complain about how he was too tired at night to do anything with his wife. Then they'd go back, work slowly, and scare each other to death about falling in. At home Walter's hands vibrated. After washing off caked–on dust, he ate twice the usual supper.

When the rest of the crew was about a hundred yards further down the road, the Polish foreman started telling Walter and Lennie what a good idea it was to get a college education. At a hundred and fifty yards he sent his cousin, a strapping black–haired fellow who worked half nude, together with four other men to finish the job. They weren't scared of falling in. They had no trouble with iron rod re–enforcement bars. They bulled together like a bunch of football linebackers and pushed the concrete around like dirt. Two hours later the collector sewer was rubble. The next day Walter and Lennie Cuppola were laid off.

It could have been worse, Walter told himself. As it was he'd put aside a few hundred dollars. Added to what he'd already saved, it was enough for a trip out west. And west was where he wanted to go. Wasn't that where young men were *supposed* to go anyway? Hadn't Huckleberry Finn gone west after all his adventures were over? The Rockies, Vancouver Island, even what the Ontario tourist bureau Heritage Map had labelled *The Champlain Fur Route* through North Bay, it all appealed to Walter. He pictured the door coves of his dilapidated British mini laden down with apples and pipe tobacco. What was there to keep him?

His mother fell silent when he told her of his plans. She couldn't do anything. Walter was stubborn.

His father thought the whole idea nuts. "Why don't you find yourself another job instead of farting about on the highways?" he asked.

Walter liked to ignore these kinds of comments.

His father's parting fusillade was: "I hope to hell you get your hair cut before you leave at least, so's you can see the bloody traffic coming at you. Goddamned menace, that's all."

Walter ignored that too.

The next morning, relieved, excited, following every curve with the seat of his pants, breathing every breath, Walter Taylor was on his way. He took a bite from a huge red–delicious apple. How tight and neat the steering of his car was! He'd whistle an aria from *The Marriage of Figaro* and imagine himself saving Mozart from penury. Then he'd drink a long inexpressibly wonderful drink of coffee from his thermos. Two hours of Canadian midsummer later he'd reached the outskirts of Ottawa. It was there that he met Nathalie Doroshkov.

She was hitch–hiking, not an unusual circumstance in itself in those years, except that she seemed a bit odd: not at all hippy–like, no long pioneer skirt—a trim, orderly figure in black who stood by the side of the road with such an extravagantly erect bearing that she looked, as someone once said, as though somebody'd stuck a pickle up her ass. Walter hesitated when he first saw her, so much so that she had to walk fifty yards or more down the highway before she got to the car, since he hadn't had the presence of mind to back up. When he finally did open the door for her, she cast him an appraising glance, lodged her black shoulder bag carefully in the back, then fairly collapsed into the front seat.

"Oh, I thought I would go mad!" she said. "Do you

realize that? I mean the people in this country must be mad!"

Walter looked at her with a little concern.

"Don't don't mind me," she continued, laying her head back and covering her brow with her hand. "Please just drive wherever you're going," and when Walter obeyed, she instantly recovered herself, sat up, and fixed him as though he were some sort of culprit.

"Do you realize how many of those big trucks tried to pick me up back there?" she demanded. "Four! And two of them wouldn't go away. They just stayed there waiting for me to get in. Can you imagine?"

Walter looked politely incredulous.

"Of course I didn't go with them, but then one of them started swearing at me. I thought he'd gone mad! He just kept swearing. I thought he would back the truck over me! Excuse me, I've got to take one of these." She shook a salmon–coloured pill into her palm from a tiny silver pillbox, clapped the pill into her mouth with a sigh, then slumped back into her seat. "Do you mind if I sleep?" she asked.

For the few moments they rode in silence, Walter took the opportunity to steal a few sidelong glances. He found her attractive, unusual, but pretty enough, and dressed entirely in black that contrasted almost too deliberately with her moled, whitish complexion.

"Where are you going?" she asked, noticing his looks. Quite unexpectedly, she extended her hand. "My name is Nathalie Doroshkov."

"Walter. Walter Taylor," he mumbled as he took his eyes off the road. Her hand felt faint and slight in his unnaturally angled grasp.

"And where did you say you were going?" she asked.

"Actually, I was travelling west."

"Oh, you too!" she laughed. All traces of her former distress had vanished. "It seems everyone is going there this year."

"Is that so?"

"Oh, yes. But I much prefer Europe."

She made this last pronouncement with the slightly clipped accent of an English governess—an affectation, Walter thought, since she'd been able to talk perfectly normally before. But he decided not to carp, even when she managed to get him to confess that he'd never been to Europe.

"Do you realize this will be the first summer I haven't seen the continent since I was fifteen?" she asked after a pause. "I can't understand how you can stay away!"

Walter shrugged.

"I don't know," he said. "Money, I suppose."

"Oh, that's nothing. I never have any. Besides, here you are travelling west as you put it, when you could be visiting interesting places, Italy, Greece, wonderful life instead of all this scenery and these hamburgers."

She made a face.

"Oh, really now. If it's so dreadful, why are you still here?"

"Believe me I wouldn't be if I could help it! What I wouldn't give to be in Venice right now. Or Florence! Imagine Michelangelos in the squares or Botticellis in the museums. So wonderful! But unfortunately my parents went and bought a cottage near Georgian Bay and I have to help them with it. I'm so depressed. I was going to go to Sweden, and now I'll have to spend at least a month in the Ontario wilderness because they don't know what else to do with their money."

Walter couldn't help smiling.

"Well, your parents seem to be doing all right to me," he finally advanced, as modestly as he could.

"Of course that's what you would think. But neither of my parents is really happy here, you know. My mother, who spent years in France, couldn't talk to the neighbours because she says she couldn't understand what they were saying. And of course there are no cafés where we were living, no *bistros*—just little French Canadian restaurants. *Chez Emile. Chez Paulo.* It's true! I'm not exaggerating. And you don't consider how ill living here has made my father. In the Soviet Union he was an accredited engineer. Here they refused to recognize him and forced him to shovel snow off the street. Can you imagine?"

"That's a shame," said Walter.

"It's not just a shame. It's dreadful! Awful! All I know is that my father doesn't want to die in this country, and I dare say I agree with him. I want *my* ashes spread on the Mediterranean."

"On the Mediterranean?"

Walter heard the note of incredulity in his voice rise a tone or two higher.

"Yes! Don't you think it would be superb? The cesspool of civilization! I even have the island picked out. When I die, my friends will all gather on the coast of Greece—everyone I have known. My best friend has promised she will take my urn, then swim to the beach at Delos, and from there scatter my ashes on the waves so everyone can see. Isn't that wonderful? Don't you think you would come?"

"Come?" Walter said with a smile. "Well, I suppose. If you're inviting me."

He rolled down the window. The rain that had been momentarily threatening had entirely disappeared. In its place was that same hot, frowsy summer day filled with the scent of exhaust and the heavy smells that issued from some dusty, vetch–infested scrubland bordering the highway. Every so often they passed the remains of an early settler's attempt to make a go of his concession, a stone grey cabin, four sheets to the wind, surrounded by the junk trees that had moved in once the evergreens had been cut and nothing else would grow.

Such a strange person, Walter thought, as Nathalie sat clutching her pill–box or brushing wisps of almost white–blond hair from her face. It turned out that her parents were not Estonians. She had told him this at first, then announced later that she was a White Russian. Since Walter didn't entirely understand the difference he let that pass. Her family had come from a region around Minsk— at least that's what she said, her father having escaped from the army in 1942, wandered into North Africa, then married a fellow country–woman he'd met in Ardennes five years later and emigrated to Canada. It was supposed to have been Brazil, Nathalie seemed delighted to add, but they'd missed that boat.

This much she told him. But what he couldn't make out, as he listened and judged, was how someone with so many pretensions and such a studied hauteur could at the same time be so bizarrely frank and such an incredible chatter–box. It wasn't that she answered his polite questions about Botticelli with rapturous talk about the poses of the angels in the Mystic Nativity or that she revealed to him, luxuriously, that yes, she loved ballet and that yes, she danced, and couldn't he tell? What really set him back were the other stories. Could he separate himself from what he said so completely as she could? Couldn't! He was weighed down with a native reserve which, under her example, he began to think he should have strangled and thrown away long ago like a dead chicken. What a talent for eliciting confessions she had too! In the wayward, casually batty atmosphere she managed to evoke, Walter found himself telling her all about Helen Morris, Madame de Bissonet, and the perils of a suburban upbringing, which he took great care to emphasize.

However nothing he could say had a patch on her. She told him of her besetting neuroses, her own incipient 'madness.' Finally she launched into a series of monologues about her lovers. She listed off the merits of her lovers' penises—blunt, squat ones, wiry ones, circumcised ones. She expatiated on her ulcer, the state of her digestion, all with a passion for self-revelation he didn't know whether to admire or deplore. When they reached Pembroke an hour and a half later, she'd depleted even her remarkable store of nervous energy and grown steadily morose, whereupon, upset by her sudden change of mood, Walter began wondering if he'd been sympathetic enough about what she'd been telling him. Out of the blue she announced she was starving.

"I have to eat something," she declared. "Could we stop, do you think?"

"Yes, of course," said Walter. "There's a restaurant back about a mile."

"Oh, no. I can't eat in a restaurant. It makes me sick. Let's go to a grocery store."

Going into a store seemed to tap new sources of energy for Nathalie Doroshkov. Her face set as she examined the food. When Walter put two vaguely bruised tomatoes in the shopping cart, she promptly put them back and complained briskly about rotting produce. It was an affront, she said. They didn't do things like that in France. She bought brie, which Walter didn't admit he disliked, then got snippy when the manager said he didn't carry *baguette*. He was the one—a peaceful old Presbyterian. She asked him why his unsalted butter was so stale (she'd stripped the foil), whereupon the old man shot Walter a glance of mixed bewilderment and commiseration. What could he do? Walter pretended not to notice.

When finally they set out a blanket in a field, she ate next to nothing. The tomatoes were floury, the cheese over–ripe; the bread tasted too much of chemicals. Then while Walter ate his share (pickily, out of deference), she began to roll slowly about in the grass.

"Oh, I have such a stomach ache," she said, holding her sides. "I shouldn't have eaten anything."

"Can I get you something?"

"No, no. It's all right." She stopped in the grass and lay back. "It must be my ulcer. I'm so nervous these days I don't know what to do. Could it be because I'm unhappy do you think?" She sat up without waiting for an answer.

For a moment they sat in silence, Walter watching a few light planes land and take off from an airstrip across the highway. Sparrows quarrelled aimlessly around a rock.

Suddenly Nathalie turned toward him. "Do you want to go to Toronto?" she asked.

"What?"

"You don't have to, you know," she quickly added. "If you would rather go out west right away you needn't worry on my account. But I'm just so depressed about visiting my parents, and I have some friends in Toronto I'd really like to see—I thought perhaps you wouldn't mind going that way." She smiled engagingly as she said this. Walter thought immediately about her stack of lovers.

"Well, I—I don't know," he said, taken aback. "Is it far from here?"

"Oh, a few hundred miles, I'd say.... But, please, don't upset your plans if it's a bother—"

"Oh, no. No bother, really. It's just that I wasn't sure about the distance—"

Why was he nattering about the distance? He knew perfectly well how far it was to Toronto.

"Well?" he heard her say after a moment.

Walter looked gravely at his watch. No, he saidt to himself. It couldn't be what he was thinking. He probably just didn't understand her. He decided to be very deliberate.

"I suppose there's no reason why not," he began very slowly. "But look, it's after four." He pursed his lips and shook his head as he looked up at her, mustering as much solemn ingenuousness as he could. "We can't possibly make it this evening."

"Oh, don't worry about that!" she replied. "Don't you have a tent?"

"A tent?"

"Yes! I'm rather like a kitten, you know. If you just give me a little corner where I can curl up, I'll be fine."

Walter was even more perturbed. It *was* what he was thinking! "My god," he said to himself. "What else could it be?"

iii

NATHALIE DOROSHKOV had a plan. They would drive until dusk, sleep over in the tent (a large, family size borrowed from his parents, as it happened); then the following morning Walter would take her to her friend's farm northeast of Toronto. All fine by Walter, to be sure. He couldn't believe his luck. But when they got back into the car and started driving, he became tongue–tied. He wasn't certain of the proper way to behave with someone like this. Did he smile at her? Put his hand on hers? In the end he decided to do nothing. He would wait for the moment when they started putting up the tent, though that proved to be no better. He was awkward, over–solicitous. She seemed to be laughing at him, so he retaliated by becoming dour. Worst of all, she was as good as her word. She spread out a little blanket at the front of the tent, declined his offer of an air mattress, and lay down for the night. Walter heard nothing more from her.

"Damn you, idiot!" he sworer at himself over and over. He couldn't sleep. Something in the tent seemed to concentrate itself on its own accord and vibrate like a soundless tuning fork. Maybe she was an insomniac? Her back was towards him, and yet he was sure she was watching him. Then there was that derelict feeling that kept bothering him. Wasn't it obvious? What more could he ask? Here was an attractive girl he'd talked to all day long, who had literally invited herself into his tent, and who was now sleeping not more than a yard away, and shamefully he hadn't made a single move. She was probably lying there waiting for the least thing, for some infinitesimal sign. They might already have been *mating like doves!*—a phrase Walter particularly liked and which he'd picked up reading the plays of George Bernard Shaw.

His imagination began to work. He started to conceive of this as a kind of duty he was meanly shirking, the way he sometimes thought after he'd masturbated too much and remembered the little homily from St. Augustine about the youth wasting his seed when there were so many young women around anxious to have it. His seed. Another of the great myths of ancient times. It was women who had seeds. All men did was fertilize, like throwing a pile of earth on an onion. Walter clapped his head against his pillow. Idle thoughts and snatches of conversation kept running through his brain. Then at around midnight, he heard the determined rustling of bedding. Nathalie's blanketed body moved dimly towards him.

"I'm cold," she said. "Do you mind if I sleep away from the door?"

She laid her sleeping bag down and huddled up beside him without waiting for an answer, her back towards his head. Walter felt a clutch of fear in his stomach. So this was what was in the cards! She would provoke him till she had the right to ask if there was something the matter with him.

Her bare shoulder was no more than two feet from his own. It was white in the moonlight that shone through the window netting, an odd alabaster white, housebred, almost medieval in its pallor, vaguely repellent. Walter wondered if he ought to reach out and touch it. Maybe she *was* cold and just wanted to get away from the door. He imagined her indignation. and felt mortified in advance. But he didn't go to sleep. Instead he turned toward her shoulder and began concentrating on it, hardly knowing what he expected to gain—perhaps under the intensity of his will to get her to turn toward him like a paper–clip on a coffee table. For a full ten minutes he gazed at her shoulder, absorbing pores, memorizing texture, until it began to resemble an alien project, a disembodied prize, and he to feel the same morbid compulsion towards it he'd felt the few times he'd set a mousetrap. He wanted to touch it, just to see. At the same time, he was scared.

He hesitated a moment, then developed his strategy. He turned deliberately in his sleeping bag as though he were adjusting his position, then brushed his hand gently across the top of her shoulder as he moved.

Nathalie bolted upright.

"What was that!"

Walter jumped.

"Sorry," he added hastily. "I guess I must have bumped into you while I was turning."

[31]

"Oh, thank god. I was having a terrible nightmare. I dreamt somebody was chasing me. Do you think we're safe in this place?"

"Oh, yes. I don't think you have to worry."

"You can't *imagine* how I hate sleeping in tents."

Walter apologized again, turned toward the wall, and tried to sleep. Underneath he felt quite relieved, though he also felt rather incompetent. Maybe there *was* something the matter with him, he thought. How was it he didn't have any of the personal dynamism he'd read about? How come red-headed whores didn't automatically stroll over to *his* table—*pour toi, c'est gratuit, cheri*—and relieve him of all his petty sexual responsibilities? Obviously he hadn't yet reached the proper peak of refined energy. Perhaps what was needed was more study, deeper application—at what, he couldn't say. He imagined his own naive face. How he must look, innocent as a lamb! He wanted to become thirty. *Fecit potentiam.* He dreamt of being thirty.

iv

NATHALIE DASHED down a small orchard road toward a figure on a stone fence. Briefly, they embraced.

"Walter!" she called, beckoning. "Come on!"

Diffident, slightly embarrassed, Walter Taylor ducked between two low–hung apple branches and walked over, eyeing a large farm dog that was circling Nathalie and her friend.

"Walter, this is Helmut Rutner," Nathalie declared in her effusive way.

Walter nodded, looking inquisitively at the long straw the other young man held in his teeth. He was always surprised by the difference between people described and people in the flesh. He always felt they were so much more themselves, so intensely *there* when first he met them. This Rutner, whom Nathalie had briefly sketched for him, was in his early twenties, moderately tall, and dressed in a baggy pair of brown corduroy pants. His face was stubbled by a day or two's growth, black like his eyebrows and darker by far than the fair copperbrown hair that hung floridly over his shirt collar. Helmut shook hands with him, then looked impatiently toward the field.

"Look, you're just in time. Allenby has The Leipziger out."

He pointed toward the pasture before them where a small herd of milk cows stood thirty yards away. It was a few seconds before Walter realized that The Leipziger was a bull. It stood toward the center of the herd, licking a cow's spine, its member like a viscous root, alternately appearing and disappearing into the folds of its body.

"Jesus Christ! Beautiful!" yelled Helmut gleefully, clapping Walter on the back.

Every so often the bull would take time out from licking, nip the cow's haunches, then make an abortive attempt to mount. At this point, Helmut would yell out encouragement, but the cow would simply take two steps toward another patch of grass, and The Leipziger would fall away, its muddy hooves scraping her flanks. Walter watched silently, thinking of the bull's enormous weight, its great eyes loaded with bovine sentiment. He kept watching until another cow, excited by what was happening, made a playful little run at him. Walter backed off the rock. At that moment Helmut Rutner threw his cap into the air, laughed uproariously, caught it, and bounded off down the road, his dog leaping up and nipping his elbows.

"Aeee–yooo!" he yelled. "Haaa–aa!"

"What's with him?" Walter asked.

"Isn't he superb?" declared Nathalie.

Walter looked at her and frowned.

The property wasn't large, less than seventy-five acres, but it contained some orchard land, enough pasture for a few head of milk cattle, a fairly large bee–yard, and a standard white frame house, all standing in the midst of the cedar brakes sixty miles northeast of Toronto. The only occupant was Helmut Rutner. The farm had been deeded to him in trust by his parents after his father had decided Canada was too harsh a place for his tastes and moved back to his native Holland. Helmut now divided his time between caring for the property and editing a small poetry magazine. Later in the kitchen, surrounded by a raft of unwashed cups, boxes of undistributed publications, and some odd, darkened honey–frames, Rutner made them all tea.

"What a wonderful place you have here," Nathalie exclaimed as she walked admiringly round a blackened wood–burning stove.

"Sit down. Sit down," said Helmut. "Make yourself at home."

Walter sat near the table and glanced up at the top of the walls where two or three large pieces of cardboard hung. On these someone had pinned various relics, chipmunk and squirrel pelts, the tailfeathers of an owl, all in neat rows, all labelled.

"Products of my hunting days," said his host as he saw Walter's glance. "But I don't do that any more." He set a heavy tea–tray down before him. "Didn't find it affirmative enough."

"Oh?"

Helmut nodded.

"It was one of those things I found I had to go through, though," he said, reaching into the refrigerator. "Get rid of my inhibitions about death." He set a little porcelain jug in front of Walter and paused, as if waiting for some elaborate confirmation. "I learned a lot," he finally added. "Things people around here don't bother about."

Helmut took a chair, reached up, and unpinned a pair of starling's wings.

"Here," he said, showing them to Walter. "See the colour of these in the light? Like oil on the street. Very beautiful," he murmured, ruffling the feathers and soothing them back into shape. "Very beautiful." He went back to his seat. Walter felt as though he'd just been offered the chance to take part in a rather special communion.

"So you enjoy it here?" he remarked blandly.

"Oh, yes."

Helmut straddled his wooden kitchen chair wrong–way–round and rested his chin on the back, determined to pursue his insight.

"Hunting concentrates the awareness like that," he said. "I don't need it any more, but it helped. I find I have to burn through to different levels all the time, you know. Sharpen perception." He got up to put the bird's wing back in its place. "Keep the blood flowing."

He said all this with a certain gravity, as though he were letting Walter in on the first principles of an orthodoxy that struck very deep and where few before him had cared to venture. Walter felt oddly flattered.

"Have you been here long?" he asked.

"Two years now. It's been that, eh Nathalie?"

Nathalie looked up from where she had been playing with the dog. She shrugged.

"Sure. About two years. Fantastic place, really. These past few months—very intense, very productive. Lots of time, peace and quiet. A lot of good poems." He shook his head as he reached for his mug. "I need a lot of time, you know. I figure at least a hundred hours per line."

Walter was suitably impressed.

"Yes, Nathalie mentioned you wrote poetry," he remarked.

Helmut nodded, as though this were to be expected. "You been here before?"

Walter looked up.

"You mean around Toronto?"

"Yes."

Walter shook his head.

"Well, it's not too bad. A long way to go, of course, but it's getting there."

"What do you mean?"

"The history of the place," he replied, glancing at Walter very appraisingly. "Too many protestants. Too many self-protective academics. I don't know what causes it. Climate, maybe. All like bugs under a rock, mining away." Helmut took a sip of his tea. "Even Nathalie here," he said, reaching over and touching her arm. "Ever see anything as white as that? Too much time in the ballet studio."

"Oh, Helmut," Nathalie laughed, promptly disengaging herself. "You must always pretend to be the Philistine. I know you spend most of your time in front of the typewriter." She turned to Walter. "Do you know he carries his manuscripts around in a black bag because he's afraid his house will burn down?"

Rutner stroked his bearded face and eyed her playfully.

"And where is your lemon, Helmut. You know I hate these awful English habits of yours."

Helmut got up from his chair.

"Your problem, Nathalie," he said as he brought her a plate and a knife, "is a lack of horseback riding. Every dancer should be made to take horseback riding. Half hour a day. Get them on the back of a good horse, put them in touch with real life. Worth fifty corrections at least."

Nathalie coloured and smiled. The dog got up, wagging its tail, and settled itself down on Helmut's foot.

"You know what I go to the ballet for?" he finally said, tickling the dog's ear. "Smell the sweat. That's the best. Good dancers sweat."

"*I* wear perfume," Nathalie declared, but Helmut paid no attention to her.

"Look at that," he mused, stroking the dog's hind leg. "See the beautiful little cunt this bitch has? It's no wonder they're all after her." He moved his hand closer to its crotch, brushing the tail aside. "All cunt is beautiful," he said as he fingered the tiny black hole. "Like a little black flower, isn't it? Just like a flower."

That afternoon Helmut organized dinner, praising himself for the fish he'd bought that morning, and following this with a long discourse on the wholesome nature of his diet, which he implied had a great deal to do with his own spontaneity and vigour of perception. Nathalie, however, quickly displaced him from the hibachi and set him to work tearing lettuce while they traded stories about the latest nutritional fraud committed by the supermarkets. At one point it turned out Helmut had been a great advocate of shoplifting and deliberate spoilage, but the farm had mellowed him, as he put it, and enabled him to take an attitude of *noblesse oblige*. Walter, who'd agreed to stay the night, was moving some gear into an upstairs bedroom.

"So," said Helmut expansively later as they were outdoors eating. "No children by your Polish lover yet?"

He had been pouring wine all during the meal, letting the liquor flow over the rim and remarking on the beauty of the red drops against the grass. Now he quaffed back his glass and sat like the gentleman in Manet.

"I don't want any children," said Nathalie.

"Jesus!" Helmut looked over to where Walter was sitting.

Walter shrugged and pretended not to be interested.

"His name is Casimir, by the way, Helmut, and you don't have to act like that," said Nathalie.

"Who's acting like that? How old is the guy, anyway? I hear he's an academic."

"He *happens* to be 43 and you know very well he's a professor."

"Jesus." He poured himself some more wine. "So how come you don't want any children?" he asked after a moment's silence.

"Why should I want children?" she replied. "Besides, I don't want to ruin my body."

"What do you mean ruin your body?"

"Well, of course it will ruin your body. What do you think? Haven't you ever seen women with two or three children? Why do you think their husbands have mistresses?"

"Bullshit!" exploded Helmut. "All these twentieth century women, so bloody skinny and neurotic. Nothing's more beautiful than a pregnant woman. Goddamn beautiful!"

Nathalie shrieked with laughter.

"Why, that's preposterous, Helmut," she said. "How would you like to have a swollen belly and big tits?"

Helmut Rutner swirled his wine in his glass.

"That's just self-hatred, Nathalie," he said darkly. "Very unhealthy."

"Oh, don't patronize, Helmut," Nathalie retorted. "You men are all alike with your obsessions. Thank god I don't have the problem. I'd cut them off entirely if only I could, they're so ugly. I find nothing worse than a woman in tights with her big boobs flopping up and down."

Helmut looked over toward Walter and shook his head. He turned back to Nathalie.

"Tell me something," he said with an ingratiating, clinical tone. "What does your Polish boyfriend think of this?"

Nathalie looked at him contemptuously.

"My Polish boyfriend, as you persist in calling him, thinks having children is perfectly ridiculous."

Helmut nodded sagely.

"Well, *you* have them if you want them so much! Why should I participate in a sick joke? Tell me that. It's alright for you. Oh, yes. You don't have to carry this thing around inside of you for nine months. But we have to have periods every month and suffer labour pains and we're supposed to feel reverence. Well, thank you *very* much."

"That's the trouble with these theoretical women," retorted Helmut for Walter's benefit. "All this French negativism—existentialism, structuralism. Horsepiss. Since when is fecundity a sick joke?"

"Well, if you can explain to me why I should spend nine months of my life creating my own replacement," Nathalie said, "then I should be very grateful. I have enough problems worrying about my own death without adding someone else's."

"You see?" said Helmut triumphantly, looking over toward Walter for confirmation.

"What?" said Nathalie.

"Parisian sickness. All those ulcerated professors' heads you've been hanging around, bleeding and complaining. All rotten with morbidity and self-devouring."

"I don't care what you say, Helmut," Nathalie replied coolly. "Perhaps *you* should have a period once or twice in your life just to see if it suits you."

"Look. There are too many women alienated from the natural process already," said Helmut. "Too much critical spirit. Very damaging. These days you have to be like Blake. Get some big Kate, teach her to read—just a bit— a little drawing. Let her get her knowledge from the earth. Intuition."

"Blake's wife didn't have any children, as I recall," said Nathalie with sarcasm.

"Doesn't matter. At least she was illiterate."

He reached over and poured Walter some more wine.

For his part, Walter wasn't saying much. He felt ill at ease. He sat back in the grass fingering the stem of his wine glass and either looking out past the barn toward the lowering sun or watching a group of ants scurry amongst a few stalks of grass. He wasn't sure he liked Nathalie's friend. Once or twice he'd been caught staring, and Helmut had stared back, only briefly, but with a certain impenetrable insolence that contrasted with his bluff, self-consciously hearty manner and gave him a look of shrewdness. Walter wondered if Nathalie had seen this and remembered she had called him superb. How could she find him superb? Outrageous, maybe. And yet he felt Rutner might have guessed something about him, and it made him confused and at the same time curious about his judgements and about the source of his confidence.

Then he found himself asking what friendship Nathalie and Rutner could possibly have had, so prone to arguing as they were. Maybe Rutner was on her scurrilous list of penises? It was a connection Walter had found himself only recently making, the instant liaison—two people talking, two people in bed. So matter of fact. She'd made it easy enough to believe this of her, though she was a born exaggerator—the pianist in Leningrad he remembered she had told him about in the car, the one who'd taken her in for a month after her visa had expired. Was it possible? He found himself staring at her while, cross–legged in the grass, she disputed with Helmut, and his gaze slipped to the trim fold of black corduroy where her thighs met. So there was the center of attraction, he thought blandly, the crux of her stories. He contemplated it as though it weren't a part of her, a separate entity, and wondered what it had been like for her, the twenty men—was it twenty?—each separate moment of possession, the intense genetic branding. Was it a weapon for her then? Or a mouth. Maybe she swallowed them, each hard, slightly ridiculous biological symbol, the crude–hatted little biological man, strangely foetal, the male rudiment. That was manhood for her, he concluded, twenty kinds of semen pullulating just under her stomach, each a part of her history, and all of a sudden the thought frightened him. Such strange brotherhood she conferred! No wonder men closed ranks against women, so vulnerable as they perceived themselves. Secretly that was what Helmut was suggesting, to close ranks against her.

"So that is what you want, Walter, some big Kate to mother you?"

He was suddenly conscious of Nathalie's question and the mocking, humorously malicious tone. He thought of Helen.

"No," he said off–handedly. "I don't think so."

"There. You see?" Nathalie turned flushing toward Helmut, her eyes laughing with victory. "At least one person here has brains."

Helmut grinned a broadening grin and winked at him.

"After that the traffic noises became raw,
the moonlight unusually intense...."

v

WALTER SLEPT THAT NIGHT in a small upstairs bedroom, the sole piece of furniture an old
puce–coloured sofa sprung with what felt like a rank of
skewers. Once during the night the sound of the passing
traffic lulled him into thinking he was home. The illusion
was so intense it took him a few moments to realize that
this was a different place, once he'd woken up from the
discomfort of his bed. After that the traffic noises became
raw, the moonlight unusually intense. He heard an irritating bird singing, though it was nowhere near dawn. He
awoke the next morning to the sound of Helmut whistling
and clattering about in the kitchen.

"Good morning!" said Rutner. "I'm just making
breakfast. Come on in."

Walter walked over and looked into the frying pan.

"Ever see eggs like that? Red. Like blood." Helmut
prodded them with a spatula. "Where's Nathalie?"

"I don't know," said Walter as he sat down at the table. "Still in bed I guess."

Helmut shook his head. "Just like her to spend half the morning in bed. Like some Russian princess." He carried the frying pan over to the counter. "Me, I believe in the sun. Me and the Greeks. Big bearded sun in the sky, good horseflesh under your ass. You like them this way?"

He showed Walter the eggs, sunny–side up.

"Sure," said Walter. "That's fine."

"There's fresh bread there. Here. Try some of this."

Walter took a piece and buttered it. Helmut gnawed off a corner and smiled at him as though the bread were a conspiracy between them.

"Going out riding after this," he said between mouthsful. "Want to come?"

Walter looked a little pained. "Well, I don't know," he said reluctantly. "I've never ridden before."

"No problem."

Helmut downed his coffee.

"Have you got another horse?" Walter asked.

"Sure, sure. We can get old Allenby's mare down the road. What do you think?"

"Well—"

Walter screwed up his face.

"Has he made you his *petit déjeuner avant l'équitation?* "

It was Nathalie. She smelt the frying pan then walked over to the mirror above the washstand and began brushing her hair.

"Yes," said Walter, tipping back his chair. "Helmut just asked me to go riding with him, but I don't think I'd be very good. What about you? Do you ride?"

"No use asking her," Helmut snorted. "She hates horses."

Walter shot her a glance.

"Do you really?"

"I most certainly do," she cried. "They're quite disgusting in the long run. All that mess they make. And they're so unpredictable."

"Nonsense," said Helmut.

"I wouldn't talk if I were you," she said in a little singsong voice. "You should show Walter that scar you got."

"Ah, that was nothing."

He didn't elaborate.

"Did you get kicked?" Walter asked after a moment.

Helmut shrugged, displeased with this turn in the conversation.

"No, it was nothing, really."

"It was *so* something," Nathalie insisted as she tugged at a tangle in her hair. "He was feeding his horse and it stepped on his foot. His toe was entirely black. It was quite frightening, really."

Helmut ignored her.

"I want to avoid the sedentary life," he said, getting up from the table. "You know Flaubert worked three days on a single sentence? Great master, Flaubert, but too sedentary. Lived too much with his mother." He knelt down to zip up his boot. "Why don't you come down to the brook later on, Nathalie?"

"Sure!"

"You too," he said, addressing Walter.

The screen door banged shut. Walter watched him

gouge some dried mud from the underside of his boot onto the verandah then make for the barn. Nathalie was still fiddling with her hair at the mirror. Even though only the day before he had been talking with her about what seemed to him the most intimate things, Walter wasn't sure now how to resume the conversation, especially how to steer it in the directions he wanted most—to find out what her relationship was with Helmut or, more important still, with her Polish boyfriend. For a moment there was an awkward silence.

"So how long have you known him?" he finally asked, drinking the last of his coffee. He swallowed a little the wrong way as he said this, and only through a real effort of will did he manage to make his coughing sound as though he were just clearing his throat.

"Who? Helmut?"

"Yes," he said, smothering his voice.

"Oh, my, years! Do you know how I met him?" She adjusted the last of her bobby–pins in her hair. "It was at a ballet school in Ottawa. He came with a friend to sketch the class. Can you imagine?" She turned toward him. "He had a long red scarf wrapped around his neck and a big curved pipe in his mouth and he sat in the corner and made these *appalling* charcoal drawings. Isn't that wonderful? I mean the lines were just all over the place! And do you know what he said when I teased him about them? He said we were all trained puppets and that's why he couldn't draw us because we oppressed him so much. Ah, ha! ha! ha!"

Walter smiled vaguely.

"So he draws, too, then," he said.

"Oh, Helmut is quite the renaissance man. Look! There he is!"

Walter glanced out the window. There was Helmut, his big dog circling round him and jumping happily up at his heels. He was mounted on a great brown dray–horse rigged out with a saddle and reins and which he rode with an air of mystery and intent grandeur. Nathalie rushed out onto the verandah.

"What's his name?" she called.

Helmut turned in his saddle as he heard her and waved, then rode off toward the cedar brake some half mile north of the house. Nathalie came back into the kitchen flushed and excited.

"Isn't he superb?" she said. "He really is quite mad. Don't you think he's mad?"

Walter made a non–committal gesture.

"Oh, I must go and phone Casimir."

She ran out of the room. Musingly, Walter again looked out the window toward the path where Helmut had ridden off. He heard Nathalie in the other room quickly hang up the receiver and come back into the kitchen.

"He's not there," she said. "What am I going to do?"

Walter looked up.

"Maybe I should have gone right to my parents' place."

"Why? Is there a problem?"

"Well, I thought Casimir might be back by now—he said he would probably be coming back last night but he's not there. Oh, well." She looked up at him and her face brightened.

"Tell me," she said. "What are *you* going to do?"

"Me?"

"Yes. What are your plans? Are you going to go out west?"

"Well, yes. I suppose I will."

"Oh." There was a pause. "Well, maybe you could stay awhile. I mean Helmut's truck is in the garage and there's no way I can get to Casimir's.... Maybe you could drive me."

"Well, I don't mind, but what about Helmut? He—"

"Oh, don't worry about Helmut! Just ask him. Oh, never mind. I'll ask him! I'm sure everything will be just fine. Anyway he has a reading tomorrow night so maybe you can drive him too!" She jumped up from the table, beaming. "You have to excuse me. I'm just going to phone my parents." She ran toward the door, then stopped. "Maybe you should take a walk toward the brook. Oh, no! You can do just what you like. I'll see you later!"

After a few minutes staring out the window, Walter took her advice. He wandered outside onto the verandah, then began walking up the path Helmut had taken a few moments before. It was an intriguing path, damp, chewed up by horseshoes, and every so often filled with little mounds of horse manure, both stale and fresh. Helmut evidently used it fairly often. In its winding way it led over a few acres of unused pasture, through a low stone dividing wall at a corner of the field, and on again toward the cedar brake. In the morning sun it was very pleasant—hot, with a few sounds of bees, and the thick smell of July weeds. He stopped on a small rise from where he could overlook the cows browsing in the pasture three or four fields to the west and mused for a while about Nathalie.

How quietly delighted in herself she seemed to him, so fluent in some new self–consciousness, with her archness and her primness that seemed to say everything she ever did in her life was in the end perfectly right and correct if only looked at in the proper light. He liked her and wanted to know her better. He thought she wanted to confide in him too, although he realized she hadn't told him anything about Casimir, despite her stories.

Walter continued down the path lost in his reveries, stripping the fuzz off some stalks of cat's tail grass and chewing the tiny green ends. Soon he was near the cedar brake. A rutted farm road that seemed to follow along its borders meandered beckoningly toward the highway to the west, but it was the cedars that interested him. The path led directly into them, and the morning heat had drawn out all their fragrance. As he brushed aside a branch, the path declined down a small ravine. Some of the hoofmarks now bore water in them. Nearby he could hear the sound of the brook splashing. He rounded a bend and a small intervening boulder, then caught sight of Helmut's horse tethered to a tamarack tree and aimlessly cropping the grass.

"Hi!" Helmut shouted. "Come on in, it's great for the nerves!" He ducked under and spouted some water into the air.

Walter stepped toward the bank of the stream and stood on a rock.

"No thanks," he called out. "I'm not much of a water fan."

Helmut made a gurgling sound with his mouth. "You don't know what you're missing!" He dove under, his buttocks pale under the water, then re–appeared a few yards away. "Too cramped here, though," he said between breaths. He ducked under again and swam toward the other bank, the water lapping softly at the hair on the nape of his neck. Walter looked behind him and went to sit on a rock.

"Where's Nathalie?" Helmut called out from the other side of the stream.

"Back at the house, I think."

Helmut's head disappeared again, then shot up just beneath Walter's foot.

"Hey! Do me a favour? Get my towel out of the saddlebag there?"

"Sure."

Walter got up and approached the horse, reaching gingerly for the rein. Just as he was about to seize it, the animal made a chubbing noise through its lips and edged away.

"Just grab him by the saddle," yelled Helmut, who was watching. "Hi! Clyde! Stay still there!"

Walter reached into the bag and whisked out the towel. Helmut had emerged, dripping, from the brook. He took the towel and began briskly rubbing himself down in the sun.

"Smells good, eh?" he said, as though divining Walter's thoughts. "Real purity here, you know. Water like ice, good hot sun, maybe a few birch branches...." His voice trailed off as he took the towel and scoured away at his scalp. "That's the trouble with people around here. They don't know the real possibilities." He shook his head dolefully, then shifted to towelling down the calfs of his legs. "All constipated with nausea and anxiety.... You take

Nathalie now. A real twentieth century woman. With someone like that you got to be quick, alert." He feinted two or three times and threw a few jabs at some imaginary opponent. "Ever heard of Catherine the Great?"

Walter looked up quizzically.

"You know she'd line up all the hussars outside her palace? The one with the frothiest pee'd have to come up and screw the old bag in her bedroom. That's right! Then they got their heads lopped off—smack! Just like that."

Helmut brought the side of one hand down against the other.

Walter smiled. "Come on," he said.

"No kidding. God's truth. You know she died screwing a horse? Some contraption rigged up with wires. Tore herself up to here." He stuck his finger on his Adams–apple. "But don't get me wrong," he said. "She's a very aesthetic girl, Nathalie. Very sensitive. Real instinct for physical grace. Physical grace—some people have it, you know." He took a few more shadow jabs. "But with a little female stinger. Little mosquito stinger."

He shook a few bits of cedar leaf from his towel and began folding it up.

"What do you know about this boyfriend of hers?" asked Walter.

"Not much. Just that she's been living with him off and on. Some forty–three year old guy—Polish, I think, from the States. He teaches here, linguistics, semantics, crap like that."

"I thought she was working in Ottawa."

"No, no. She's all over the place." He buckled up the saddlebag and went to untether his horse. "Look, Nathalie tells me you're going out west?"

[53]

"That's right. I thought I would."

"Good plan, man. But you're welcome to stick around for a while if you like. Go into town, have a look around. See, I have this poetry reading this week and my truck's in the garage. I've got to check on it now as a matter of fact, but the guy said two days, so—"

"Yes. Nathalie mentioned it. If it's a question of a lift, that's no problem."

"Good! That's good! Look, it's at eight, the day after tomorrow. We can leave here about an hour and a half beforehand."

After a pause Walter looked up at him and asked, "What is it you're going to read?"

Helmut seemed delighted with this question.

"Rasputin," he replied. "Ever hear of Rasputin?"

Walter nodded.

"Fantastic man, Rasputin. Real prophet." Helmut Rutner fiddled with his stirrups. "You know he used to talk to all the horses? All the animals. Ten years old, he picked out a horsethief just by looking at him. Just like that. Fantastic! Best stuff I've written so far, maybe the best in Canada. Shit! *Canada!* Bloody world premier! Knock the little bastards right out of their pants."

Rutner jumped into the saddle.

"Hey! What do you think of this?—Rasputin's hair. Stunk like hot sheep's cheese." He chortled gleefully. "Like hot sheep's cheese! Jesus!"

Walter laughed as Helmut rode off. Later that evening, as he was sitting on an old bench on the verandah while Nathalie read and Helmut laboured over *Rasputin* under a gooshenecked lamp, Walter let himself relax for the first time since he'd arrived. After all, he said to himself, maybe Rutner wasn't so bad.

vi

HELMUT RUTNER'S READING was to be held in a university building called The Women's Pavilion, a worn, oak-trimmed place with ancient air–pneumatic closers at the top of the doors and rooms with large jungle–style fans slowly whirling from the ceilings. At the rear was the Lectern Salon, a medium sized room where once a month literary *soirées* were conducted. The lights were dim, intimate, and an assortment of chesterfields and hardbacked chairs lined the walls. Helmut seemed brasher than usual as he entered. He looked round impatiently. University readings weren't something he was fond of, he'd said to Walter in the car. The bugs always came out of the woodwork.

One particular specimen Helmut had already spotted, a bearded young man with round gold–rimmed glasses who was standing near a table covered with little cakes and sandwiches. He was an enemy—a rationalist and prickless snot. His name was Jonathan Styles, and the two of them had apparently spent a good deal of time devouring each other in the letters to the editor sections of various literary magazines. Styles had called Rutner an intellectual hooligan and a blood–drinker. Rutner had countered with librarian and frigid male. On this occasion, however, Helmut's attentions had been quickly engaged by an intense, dark–haired little man in a fedora who would nod appreciatively at him, then at his wife who was standing a few paces behind.

"Cut a word open and it will bleed," Rutner was saying. "Hopkins. Even bloody incredible Hopkins— smooth words, sandy words, hairy words. Jesus! A word's like an octopus, you know that? Big pulpy head, lots of tentacles, reach around, grab everything in sight."

Feeling curiously self-important, Walter never strayed very far from his friend. Since the reading didn't begin on time, he was given the chance to look over the people who had come. Nathalie wasn't there. She'd said she was tired. Besides, she hated readings. For his part, foot propped casually on the back of a chair, Walter stood very much toward the reading table, surveying the various groups with a critical eye, noting the two or three people who had been pointed out to him, Jonathan Styles, the girl he was with in a pink blouse. All in all Walter tried to look, if not like a poet who was about to read himself, then at very least like the *eminence grise* behind one who was.

Helmut was preceded by two others, the first a sensitive Trinidadian man reading from a lugubrious poem about roses and jasmine and, in the one line Walter could remember, lamenting the fact that his brain had been hung out on a line to dry. Twenty minutes later Helmut took his place under the study lamp. He seemed nervous and set out his equipment on the table very deliberately—cigars, matches, a large pocket watch—before removing a sheaf of papers from a battered schoolbag at his knee. Then he began. First he read several smaller poems, each with a personal introduction about its origins. There followed some longer works with longer personal introductions, some experiments with the villanelle, some translations from Sextus Propertius, more personal talk about his upbringing and his reading habits. Three quarters of an hour passed. With *Rasputin* (billed magniloquently as *The Rasputin Cycle: an Epic*) still to come, a certain portion of his audience had grown restive. Even Walter began to feel an anxious little void in his stomach, as Helmut's prefatory remarks grew less jaunty and more apologetic.

"Here's one you might like," he would say, as though just one more would do the trick and he could finally feel at ease. Or, with a brave attempt at candour: "This one has flaws—this is a flawed poem, but it has really good moments."

Ten minutes later, when Jonathan Styles yawned openly and placed his knuckles against his skull, Helmut understood. He pushed aside his giant clutch of poems and removed the typescript with an air of beleaguered genius. This *was* what people had come to hear, after all.

"Alright," he said, putting his hand on his watch. "This next one I've been working on for the last six months. I just want to tell you that Reynard Phelps said this was the best thing produced in Canada so far. Plus I got a letter from Louis Feinberger saying it was better than anything the old Montreal gang had ever come up with. You can all see that letter as part of the introduction to my next book."

Then he began.

"Saint, *ubermensch, bogatir!*"

He read from the section entitled 'Ode.' Helmut liked lots of passion, gesticulation. He thought of himself a bit like Yevtushenko, he'd said to Walter in the car, at heart an actor. For *Rasputin* he pulled out all the stops. There were lavish passages on thaumaturgy and inner vision, lewd scenes featuring *khlysty* sectarians and fat upholstered countesses. Rasputin was a string–bearded goat. His yellow, fish–soup body oozed a mixture of sweat and semen. This, said Helmut, was holy. This was absolution.

After a good deal more in a similar vein, Walter noticed that the conversations from the vicinity of Jonathan Styles had grown louder. There were a few "sh's" from the audience, but at the back it had become difficult to hear, just as Helmut started on the section of his poem he'd previewed for Walter in the orchard near his bee-yard that afternoon, a section that had made a peculiar impression on Walter for reasons he was unable to explain. He strained to hear as Rutner described how the lieutenants and civil servants of the capital had actually considered it an honour for their wives to sleep with a stinking monk. Actually an honour, Walter repeated to himself, and he remembered being struck by the lines that afternoon the first time he'd heard them, just as he now found himself drifting away from the poem and puzzling over them again.

How did such men feel when their wives got home, he wondered. What did they say to each other? Did they carry around a shared secret between them which they never discussed? Walter tried to imagine himself in a similar situation. Was it erotic, he asked himself, like an acquiescence, morbidly satisfying? Maybe that was the honour. Now they had a stake in power, godly sperm—a new kind of baptism. They could commune with it. And the child that might emerge from such an episode? Walter tried to imagine it, not the twoness of family resemblance but another thing sitting in their midst like a buddha, strange, alien flesh. The grunt of passion, the final unanimity. A sickly sweet sensation descended to the pit of his stomach.

Then, in the midst of a long evocation of Rasputin's death, ("manacled, gnawing his way through Moskva ice"), Walter was startled by the abrupt clattering of a chair. He turned to catch a glimpse of Jonathan Styles making for the door and clumping dramatically, conclusively, up the stairs. Helmut stopped. It was clear from the perspiration that broke out all over his forehead that he was shaken. A pause, then a voice shouted, "Oaf! Ignore him!" It was the man in the blue fedora.

"Go on! Go on!" said another. There was a burst of applause. "Bravo!"

Minutes later a smattering of people gathered to congratulate him. The little man in the blue fedora approached again. He spoke of an evening of culture, of edification.

"You're to be congratulated, young man," said the man's wife edging a little closer. "I know what it was like in that country." Turning toward the door she screwed up her nose and added, "Pay no attention to them."

"That's right! That's right! You have talent. Talent speaks for itself!"

Rutner glowed. Rutner was charming. Rutner auto-graphed a portion of his manuscript and gave it to them. He chatted to them for a quarter of an hour before he restuffed his schoolbag, but even this didn't assuage him entirely.

"Goddamn bastard!" he spat as Walter followed him up the stairs and into the street. "The little grammarian. Did you see him stomp out of there? Fucking little critic. *Jesus!* You can't do anything in this country without these spiders trying to eat you, you know that? They'll do anything. Take your stuff, spew out their dribble." Helmut shook his head. "What's that guy's ambition anyway? Three guesses what his ambition is.... *Articles!* Little bitchy articles any dung beetle could have rolled up on a hot day. No kidding! Ever seen the libraries? Maybe a shelf, shelf and a half for one of the big boys, six, seven shelves for the creeps, all gnawing and chewing away at him like tent caterpillars. And multiply! Libraries aren't big enough for them. They ought to have a big clean–up campaign. Every year the lousiest, fattest book on some guy is burnt. Creep spends five years writing his tome? Bang! Into the pile! Big public burning. Teach him a lesson. —Hey, you want a pizza?"

"What?"

"Come on, I know a good place."

They walked in silence for a while, Helmut still shaking his head to himself every now and again, then finally relaxing as he made a few jokes about the perils of early recognition and how all good work was ultimately guarded and difficult to penetrate. They walked into a small old–fashioned restaurant with high booth walls and a few old men dressed in grey and black reading newspapers at the rear. Helmut shook hands with the owner and chatted for a while as Walter waited patiently behind.

"All dressed, Rico. Anchovies, black olives. The whole works. —Fantastic people, these Italians. You know that guy reads translations of Ezra Pound?" He shook his head, and then after putting his satchel carefully in the corner of the seat, proceeded to discuss that night's reading. There were those around who couldn't fathom the complexities of the unconscious at work, it seemed. People like Styles (the real barometer) were so tight–assed they couldn't let their intuitions loose to play over the language.

"You know, sometimes I don't even know myself what an image means? It comes to me in a dream sometimes, like the one with the old man pole–vaulting over the moon. I don't know why it had to be there, but it fit. It's just got to be like that," and he went on to elaborate on his theory of private energy. The world was filled with envious and resentful leeches. Every great man attracted them by virtue of his extraordinary force and authority. And just as Walter noticed a girl in the next booth lower her fork and turn her head, the better to hear what was going on, suddenly he felt some of the pride and enthusiasm he'd felt for Rutner the previous night return. Face flushed with redoubled interest and attention, Walter leaned a little closer to his friend as though the two of them were engaged in some wonderful and intensely personal conspiracy.

"Rasputin had a friend," Helmut said. "Belly–aching, conniving back–stabber. You have to watch it. They flatter you, pretend they're your allies, then bang! You get it in the neck. Just when you least expect it."

"Excuse me," came the voice of the girl beside them. "Aren't you the poet?"

Helmut looked up.

"I'm sorry, I was at your reading before and I didn't get a chance to tell you how interesting I found it." She smiled a sweet little smile, almost from some inner prompt card. " I really enjoyed it."

Helmut nodded. It took him a moment to realize that this girl who was now talking to him was the same one who had been talking to Jonathan Styles earlier that evening. She was short. She had the same full breasts and pink blouse, the same grey tweed skirt, freckles, and reddish–brown hair. When it registered, he looked her over more curtly and addressed her with a bantering, cooler edge to his voice.

"You were the one who was talking to Styles before, weren't you?"

"Oh, Jonathan?" She seemed a bit taken aback by his tone. "Yes, as a matter of fact I was chatting with him for a while. He seemed like an awfully nice fellow." She looked over toward Walter who just shook his head as though he didn't know who she was talking about. "Very interesting, really."

Helmut's eyes narrowed as she said this, and he looked up almost superciliously toward the cloud of blue smoke from his little brown cigar.

"Well, look," he said, butting it and edging his elbow over the booth railing. "I'm always interested in a woman's reaction to my work. I find it really helps me, gives me another perspective. A bit like seeing under water, if you follow me. So maybe you could give me an idea, you know—" (he waved his hand deprecatingly to show that he didn't mean this to be at all intimidating) —"just what it was that grabbed you about it, what were the really high points."

The girl smiled slowly, put the tip of her tongue thoughtfully on her two front teeth, and tried to conceal her pleasure at being asked to do this.

"Well," she said, "I don't know. I think I liked the scene with his daughter. Yes, I liked that very much, and, well—the parts about his childhood." She was still smiling, now a little wistfully. "Yes, they were very nice, I thought." She was about to pursue this, but noticing Helmut's reaction she quickly demurred. "Although..." she drawled musingly.

"What?"

"Well, I don't know. I didn't think I liked his death quite so much."

"Oh?"

"No," she said. "I don't think I liked it."

"Why not?"

"Oh, just a feeling I guess."

For Rutner she had said the magic word. Helmut looked at her with magistral pleasure and lit another cigar.

He had begun to talk about Rasputin in connection with the mysterious dark personality 'beyond the facts' that existed in every historical figure when Rico appeared with two pizzas. Helmut picked up the salt shaker.

"What's your name anyway?" he asked.

"Judy Stoddard."

But it was clear the girl didn't want to lose the gist of their conversation, and she quickly returned to what they'd been talking about, growing more intrigued as Helmut conducted a rambling discourse on the nature of the freedom of a man of vision, and finally, with an engagingly hesitant surprise, finding herself in agreement with just about everything he had to say and thinking nothing of it when Helmut invited her to join them. Walter, who had sat listening, soon found his anchovies remarkably strong and quietly ordered another drink. Suddenly he got the urge to go to the bathroom. Moments later Helmut was in the tiny urinal beside him.

"Look," he said, "I think I'm going to go over and have a look at some furniture tonight, so maybe I can just give you the keys and you and Nathalie can look after the place by yourselves. What do you say?"

"What's this?"

"Mmm?"

"Where are you going to look at furniture?"

"Oh, Judy's friend has just moved out, got a job across town, so there are some things she wants to sell. I thought I might go over and have a look at them."

"I see," said Walter turning on the tap to wash his hands. "And how are you going to get back?"

"Don't worry. It'll be o.k."

Helmut's eyes narrowed as he said this. Walter took the keys from his hand.

"So look, don't worry," Helmut repeated as he reached for the doorknob. "You know where everything is. Allenby takes care of the cattle in the morning and...."

He shrugged.

[65]

"Of course," said Walter, a little more stiffly than he'd intended.

Helmut gave him a satisfied wink and went back to his seat.

But there was the small problem, Walter realized as he pulled at the towel dispenser, of how he was supposed to leave. Did he go up to the table, finish his pizza (which he found inedible), and make some absurd excuse? Did he shake hands with them both? In the end he decided the simplest course was best. As he opened the door, the girl looked up. He nodded foolishly and waved, paid his bill, and left.

v i i

IT WASN'T AS THOUGH Walter didn't ask himself questions about what had happened with Helmut Rutner that night. He did. Simultaneously puzzled, admiring, concerned, all the way back in the car he would ask himself what it was about Rutner. Was he handsome in some way Walter hadn't quite noticed before? The beard? Maybe it was the beard. He found himself feeling gingerly for his own smooth–shaven face. No, he declared to himself. He couldn't bring himself to believe that. He'd seen Rutner in the morning when Helmut's skin had that peculiar bloated quality, as though his body hadn't quite gotten rid of all its wastes. Often Rutner's brown eyes had a close–set, pig–like look to them. Walter felt suddenly reassured. Then he plunged again into the scene in the little pizza shop. She'd seemed a perfectly normal, agreeable sort of girl, this Judy Stoddard. He couldn't quite fathom it.

When he parked the car in Rutner's long dirt drive – way and stepped out into the cooler rural air, he stopped for a moment. The stars were immensely bright, æons closer, and the crickets throbbed in the darkness like the earth's pulse. Beyond in the shadows, loomed Helmut's clap–boarded farmhouse, lightless, alien in the moonlight, like a curious challenge. Walter peered at his keys for the right one.

When he got in the house, he decided to go and have a look down the hall and up the stairway landing. The light in Nathalie's bedroom seemed out, and he wondered if she were even there. Opposite him, below in Helmut's study, a little goose-necked lamp spread a shadowy glow over the room. Walter retraced his steps. He saw papers strewn about the desk, a heap of old clothes in the corner, some yellowed, spindly ivy plants sitting uncared for on the window–sill. He opened a cupboard door: cross–country skiing equipment, a small .22 calibre rifle, stacks of old Penthouse magazines. He flipped through a few, then walked over to the bookcase and leafed through some folders, one of which contained the typescript of an essay entitled "Hymn to Dionysus and his Maenads," and in the few paragraphs Walter managed to read, he gathered Helmut was making the connection between maenadism, premenstrual syndrome, and sudden hormonal shifts, all the while suggesting that had Tolstoy understood the link he would have conquered his gynophobia and never written *The Kreutzer Sonata*. Walter picked up a beige manilla folder. Loose papers this time, a calendar with strange notes and circled dates. Then the letters. Walter felt a thrill of perverse excitement well up in his stomach. A treasure trove! Some still in their envelopes, post-marked Holland, others dated from Montreal, Saskatoon, the Bahamas. He sat down on a rug in front of the bookcase and pulled out a snippet of blue paper. A round, childish script carried the following message:

> How is John Thomas? Lady Jane misses him, her servant, and wants him. She sends love and encouragement to him because he is her trinket and pudding.
>
> L.J.

Walter felt a flinch of embarrassment. He was tempted to put these back, but the heading of another caught his eye. Slowly he read it.

Cher Helmut,

Je viens de recevoir ta lettre! Tu m'as complètement bouleversée par ce que tu m'as écrit. Helmut, c'ést incroyable! Si j'avais su que tu réagirais ainsi, je ne te l'aurais jamais dit, je te l'assure! Maintenant je ne sais plus quoi faire. Je veux tellement aller te voir Helmut; j'ai envie de prendre le prochain autobus et te rendre visite afin de comprendre ce que tu penses de moi. C'est fini entre Fernand et moi! C'est vrai, Helmut, je te le jure! Pourquoi ne veux-tu pas comprendre que tu es le seul homme avec qui je voulais avoir un enfant? Et quant à mes folies en France, j'étais si sûre que tu m'avais comprise. C'est pour ça que je te les ai racontées. Je les regrette maintenant de tout mon coeur et tout ce qui s'est passé au cours de cette mauvaise époque—la prostituée, Pigalle, ma soumission aux exigences farouches de Jacques—toute cette histoire lamentable. Mais tu ne peux pas permettre que cela fausse notre avenir ensemble, Helmut, je t'en prie!

O, oui, je sais pourquoi tu étais faché contre moi! Je le sais trop bien. Mais je n'ai pas eu la chance de m'expliquer, Helmut. Ce n'était que le début de nos relations. Nous ne

*nous connaissions depuis à peine deux mois, et je t'ai dit
qu'il y avait des hommes dans ma vie! Mais je comprends
ce que tu disais, Helmut. Je comprends pourquoi tu as senti
une telle sympathie pour Alain, pourquoi il a decidé de fuir
la chambre quand j'ai commencé à faire l'amour avec
Claude à Lyons. Mais c'était pour rire Helmut, sans plus!
Et Alain ne savait jamais comment faire l'amour. Je pensais
que ça pourrait lui faire du bien, c'est tout. O, Helmut, je
crois de temps en temps que tu veux me rendre coupable,
comme ma mère a toujours essayé de faire.*

*Ta lettre m'a fait un choc, m'a étourdie, cependant je
n'ai pas compris une ligne de ta poésie que tu m'as citée:*

*Mad in pursuit, and in possession so;
Had, having, and in quest to have, extreme.*

Pourquoi m'as-tu écrit ça Helmut?

*O, si tu savais comme je me sens triste et laide à la fois,
tu ne m'aurais jamais refusée de te voir. De temps en temps
je pense que je quitterai Montréal, que je partirai sac-au-
dos pour me rendre n'importe où, au Mexique ou au Brésil.
Après avoir lu ta lettre j'aurais pu dire que tu es méchant
et cruel, mais je sais que ce n'est pas vrai, Helmut. Je veux
venir. Tout sera réglé! Nous serons heureux ensemble, j'en
suis sûre.*

Micheline

Walter, whose French was not especially good, had to
read the letter over two or three times before he understood
it, and even then he wasn't sure exactly what it meant. If
only there had been replies! He started to leaf through the

contents of the folder more carefully, but to no avail. "Damn," he thought to himself. He began to scan the other pieces of paper in the folder when he heard the sharp sound of the bedroom door opening, the sound of someone coming down the stairs. Quickly he put the folder back and got to his feet. Nathalie stuck her head into the room.

"Oh, it's you! Where's Helmut?"

Walter turned to her.

"Actually, he's still in town. He met some girl in a pizza place after the reading and went to look at some furniture she was selling."

"Furniture! At this hour?"

"Well, I don't know. That's what he said."

"He's gone to look at furniture!"

Nathalie laughed uproariously. "Is that what he said?"

She sat down heavily on an old rocker. She seemed to find this absurdly funny.

"Is that really what he said? Oh dear, that's price-less!" She giggled some more. "So what's her name?" she asked, becoming desperately interested.

"Judy. Something like that. Judy Stoddard."

Nathalie shrugged. "I don't know her." She glanced at her watch. "Well, look, I'm going to make milk. Would you like some?"

"No thanks."

"You should have some. I always have it at night. It makes me feel good. I sleep better."

"Really?"

"Oh, yes. Are you sure you wouldn't like some?"

"No, I don't think so. I think I'll go on upstairs myself."

"That's fine. Suit yourself."

He really didn't know why she'd laughed at Helmut's adventure. He himself found it rather admirable. To be so certain of your own abilities, to send someone home (himself) and deliberately cut off all avenues of retreat, it *was* admirable. It was raw courage! Maybe something of that sort of confidence communicated itself, he thought. There he was. Rutner. Obnoxious, irrepressible Rutner, who wasn't going to be thwarted, who didn't even take the prospect of failure into consideration. She *had* to have him. After all, these things happened. There was no denying it, especially now that he'd seen it take place before his very eyes. No signals, no special signs. No special strain or willfulness. Nothing he could put his finger on. He found the whole thing a lesson.

Walter quietly undressed and turned out the light. Nathalie was moving around in the other room, sifting through her clothes, turning the bathroom water on and off. Suddenly he heard her footsteps approaching his door. There was a knock.

"Walter? Are you in bed?"

"Yes," he answered with a questioning sound to his voice.

"Well, do you mind if I ask you something?"

She opened the door.

"No, not at all."

"You won't be mad?"

"I won't be mad," he laughed.

"How come you never brush your teeth before you go to bed? I mean here you are such a nice fellow, and you go right to bed with your teeth dirty. How can you do that? Don't you have a toothbrush?"

"Of course I have a toothbrush. I just forgot, that's all."

"How can you *forget?* Really! Let me see your teeth."

She snapped on the light and walked over to the bed.

"Come on. Let me see."

"What do you mean, let me see your teeth. There's nothing wrong with my teeth."

"Come on. Will you open your mouth and just let me see? Come on, that's it."

Walter sat up and opened his mouth.

"Turn your head a little toward the light here. No, no. The other side. There."

She cocked her head back and squinted at him.

"Do you have a toothpick?"

"Are you crazy? I don't need a toothpick."

"Just this one part! I think you have a huge cavity right in your front tooth."

"Aw, go on. It feels fine."

He closed his mouth.

"Well, you *do* have a cavity. I can see it, and if you don't do something about it you'll lose all your teeth. Besides, your breath smells. Let me see again."

He opened his mouth.

"Pooh!" she said and backed away. "Now why don't you want to go and brush your teeth."

"Alright, alright. Can I get some clothes on?"

"Certainly, I won't look."

She stood over him as he put the toothpaste on the brush.

"My dentist told me that you had to brush up and down," she said, taking her own toothbrush from a little bag. "See? Like this."

She brushed with an exaggerated didactic motion. Walter followed her.

"See how clean?" She stood on tip-toes in front of him. "Let me smell."

He returned to bed with a bland salty taste in his mouth. His gums were bleeding painlessly. In the other room he could hear Nathalie turn out her light and pull down the covers of her bed. Moments later there was another knock on his door.

"Walter?"

"Mmm?"

"Are you in there?"

She opened the door.

"Walter, I can't sleep. You wouldn't happen to have a tranquillizer, would you?"

"No."

"Well, can I come in and chat maybe? I feel lonely."

Walter sat up under the covers.

"You don't mind?"

"No, no. Of course not."

She turned on the light and came and sat down on the side of the bed.

"I'll just sit here, and we can talk for a while. There. Now what shall we talk about."

Walter rubbed his eyes from the light and looked at her blankly.

" I don't know," he said. " What would *you* like to talk about?"

"Let's talk about this bedspread. Do you know I saw a bedspread just like this one in Germany when I was there? I was staying at an aunt's (she's not really my aunt), and she had this little boy—oh, not so little I suppose, about thirteen or fourteen. Well, you've never seen such a mama's boy in your whole life. Mummy knitted him stockings, mummy made sure the holes in his shoes were fixed, and every Sunday mama made him a big huge chocolate mousse with piles of whipped cream. Well, the worst thing was he started following me *around*. I couldn't go anywhere without him being there. I'd go to the museum and there he'd *be*. Sometimes he'd try and hide and pretend he didn't know I was there, but usually I saw him. And then he started trying to buy me things. Oh, all sorts of little junk, chocolate bars, little things like that. Of course I didn't take them, but by then my aunt was starting to get suspicious. Can you imagine? I don't know what she thought—I mean he was just a *baby!* And then one time I caught him masturbating in the bathroom over my picture."

"Over your picture!"

"Yes! I can't understand where he got it. Maybe my aunt had it, I don't know, but it was all very embarrassing."

Walter found his hand remarkably near her thigh as she talked.

"It sounds embarrassing," he said gravely, realizing that if he adjusted his body to the right, he might accidently be touching her.

"Really, I don't know. I mean some *people* !"

By now Walter's heart was pounding in his chest. This *was* his opportunity after all, and yet he found the whole process so nerve–wracking he was tempted to ignore the fact that the curve of her thigh was now resting against the outer edges of his little finger, and to pretend the whole thing had been nothing more than an innocent accident. He couldn't reply to her talk any more. He knew if he opened his mouth either his breath would catch or his voice would break. Instead he opened the palm of his hand and laid it flat on her leg. Then he reached out, took her in his arms, and kissed her as tenderly and as sweetly as he knew how.

"Do you want to sleep with me?" she said.

A smile of pride and relief played across his face. "Of course!" he said.

God knew he had been gentle. He had been delicate. He had even been sentimental. When he spoke her name for the first time, he felt a sheet of tiny pinpricks of pleasure move through his stomach like an infinite series of little French pastilles. He was filled with that sense of newness and gratitude he'd once read about in Bertrand Russell. Tears had almost come to his eyes — and she'd responded by taking his lower lip into her mouth and biting it until it ached. She was like a lioness. She sucked at the soft skin around his neck and brought the blood painfully to the surface. She bit him, kissed him, stroked the back of his neck, and then all of a sudden Walter felt her feet hook themselves persistently round the inside of his shins and begin to wedge his legs apart like a tire jack. "Was this some sort of contest?" he asked himself. He resisted. She wasn't going to force his legs apart every time she felt like it. But her thigh muscles were incredibly strong, and he found he couldn't do anything to prevent it.

"Come on. Stop it!"

"What's the matter?"

"Come on, you're making me feel like an idiot."

"Aw. Baby doesn't like to do the splits?"

She caught at his legs again and moved them apart almost effortlessly. He came a few moments later in a tumult of compensatory energy.

"Well, that was quite a little burst you had there," she declared.

Walter muttered a reply, feeling richly peaceful and strangely humiliated all at once.

"I mean you moved so quickly! I've never had anyone who went that fast. You just sped right along, I had to watch you!"

Walter lay on his back, holding her hand.

"But now I'm all chatty, and you'll have to entertain me."

How did she want to be entertained, he asked himself. It was an effort to speak.

"What do you mean?"

"Well, I don't know. Maybe you can tell me things."

"Like what?"

"I don't know. Maybe you can tell me how you got de–virginized."

There was a silence.

"Well, come on. Who did it? How did it happen? Tell me."

Hesitantly, Walter told her more about Helen Morris and the canoe trip. Nathalie wasn't impressed.

"You mean you never actually got to do it with her?"

"Well, no. I suppose not."

"Ah, ha! ha! ha!" she laughed. "That's priceless. How come? Didn't you want to do it?"

"Well, of course I wanted to. But she told me she was moving away, that's all."

Nathalie laughed again.

"So I'm only your second lady?" she said.

Walter hunched up his shoulders.

"Well, that's alright. I don't mind, you know. I really don't."

Walter held her hand more firmly.

"Do you want to know how I got de–virginized?"

"Well...." He shrugged. "Alright."

"Do you really want to know?"

"Sure, sure."

"Well, you'll never guess who did it."

"Who?" he finally said, exasperated.

"Helmut Rutner."

"Helmut Rutner!"

Walter released her hand.

"Yes! What's so odd? He was a very nice boy when I first knew him."

"Oh?"

"Yes! My mother really liked Helmut. Why, she could even speak German to him. And he didn't look like he does now, you know. He dressed quite nicely really, clean, very presentable."

Walter tried to imagine Rutner with his bristling beard and his messy cigars as a nice, presentable young man.

"My mother thought he was wonderful. He even stayed in our house for a week. How come you're so stiff?"

She suddenly grabbed his leg. "Look, so rigid. You don't like me telling you these things?"

"Oh, no. I don't mind."

"Well, you *asked* me you know. I can't blot out my past."

"No, no. Of course not."

"Well, don't you want to know what happened?"

"Alright."

He turned on his side to face her, as if to say he refused to be frightened by anything she could possibly tell him.

"Well, as I say, Helmut stayed at our house for a week, and, well, I liked him and he liked me, and I had this problem about being a virgin."

Walter smiled wanly.

"Well, it's true. I was eighteen years old—or did I just turn eighteen?—I don't know. Anyway, he was there and we just did it. Right on my own bed, too. He told me to get on top of him and stick it in as far as I wanted, a little bit at a time—"

Walter made a face.

"Well, do you want to hear or don't you? I mean, really! I don't see what there is to be so ashamed about. It's just bodies."

"It's not just bodies."

"Of course it's just bodies!" she laughed. "You had your lady in a field, you know."

"Yes, yes. It's true," he said, wearily.

"Well—"

"Go on, I'm listening."

"Well, nothing. I mean he just did it, all very efficient and painless, and that was it. I was very happy about it. He told me himself he'd done me a great favour, and I really believe it. In fact, I even thanked him for it. There are some pretty terrible stories around, you know."

Walter gave her an odd look.

"Well, maybe not *terrible* exactly, but not very pleasant, you have to admit."

Walter nodded his head in assent. There were, he thought.

"And do you still...?"

Nathalie looked at him archly.

"Oh, of course not. We don't get along. I mean, we get along—we're great friends, but, well, you understand."

"How come you don't get along?"

"Well, it was so long ago. Over three years now, and I had to move around for jobs, and he got another lady. Some French girl, I think."

Walter thought immediately of the Micheline of the letters. He felt almost prescient now to have read them— and guilty too, as though he'd done his bit of preparation and was now filled with the vile little pleasure of other people's secrets.

"But that's alright," she said. "That's as it should be. Helmut liked women. He was very frank about it, and *I* certainly didn't mind. Then I had Casimir, after all."

"What. Right away?"

"Oh, no. A few months later maybe—What's this?" she said suddenly grabbing him. "Oh, it's all soft. Little babykins all soft?" she said, shaking it. "Little noodle's tired?"

Walter didn't know what to say. He had never imagined himself in bed with a woman and not being able to do anything, not carrying on all night and into the next morning as well, but here it seemed there was nothing he could do. Try as he may, all he could summon up were a few diffident pangs of pleasure, nothing more.

Nathalie yawned. "By the way," she said, rolling down the covers and taking a piece of tissue paper from under her pillow, "don't you have things?"

"Things?"

"Rubber things. Condoms."

"No, I don't."

"Well, not every girl has an iud, you know." She went to get out of bed.

"Where are you going?"

"I'm going to my room."

She bent down and picked up her nightgown. Walter felt his heart sink.

"Why? What's the matter?"

"Well, I'm sorry, I'd like to stay with you, but I can't. I can't stand anybody in the same bed with me. I can't sleep."

"Oh."

Walter looked downcast.

"But I'll come and visit you in the morning, o.k.?"

"Fine," he said, a little unhappily, and as she went through the door, he called out to her, "Hey, I want to hear about your Polish boyfriend."

"About *what* ?" she said, with some disdain.

"No. I just want to know, well— Wouldn't he be angry about what just happened?"

"Angry? Why should he be angry? He doesn't own me, you know."

"I suppose not, but I just wanted to understand — what the situation was between you, that's all."

[81]

"I see."

She turned and looked out the darkened window. Then she folded her arms across her chest and breathed out a little breath of anger and contempt from her nose.

"Casik and I had a little disagreement a while back, that's all."

"A disagreement?"

"Yes. You could call it that."

Suddenly her eyes flashed on him fiercely, as though he himself had been responsible.

"Do you realize I had to chase that stupid, horrid man with a carving knife and actually threaten him? Do you realize that? Physically threaten him?"

"What in heaven's name for?"

"Because he *lied* to me, that's why. He told me he sent a telegram to his first wife—who hates him, by the way, and won't have anything to do with him—and, well it turns out this telegram is supposed to wish her a happy birthday. And then when he saw how angry I was, he told me it was all a joke. He said he wanted to test me to make me jealous, and that he hadn't sent it at all! Can you imagine?"

"So? What did you do?"

"What do you mean what did I do? I phoned up the telegraph company and said I was Mrs. Kusiuski and did my husband just send a telegram to Prague. Well, of course he *had*, and the man told me he had. So I put down the phone and confronted him with this. And do you know what he said?"

"What?"

"He said, 'The man at the telegraph office is a liar! I never sent a telegram to Prague. He's invented the whole story.' Imagine! He thought I was an idiot. So I phoned up the telegraph man again, and I asked him if he was completely sure that a Mr. Casimir Kusiuski had sent a telegram to Prague that day and would he please read me the contents. Well, he wouldn't read them to me, but of course Casimir *had* sent it, and so I just put down the receiver and got a bread knife out of the drawer, and I told him I'd kill him."

She threw her head back and gave a loud laugh.

"Ah! ha! ha! ha! It's too incredible. You'll never guess what he did. It was lunchtime and he backed around the table with this little hard–boiled egg in his hand, all peeled and ready to eat, and he just kept *mashing* it in his hands saying, 'But darling, be reasonable! Be reasonable!' I could hardly keep from bursting out laughing. I mean there he was with his big fat stomach and this little hard–boiled egg. It was simply ridiculous!"

"So what did you do?"

"I just flung the knife across the room. Then I declared him dead. What did you expect?"

"And that was it?"

"You mean to say you want more? That wasn't enough? I detest betrayals. I loathe them. I won't stand for them. Oh, he's disgusting. Men are so disgusting!"

And she left him to turn out the bedroom light himself.

viii

WHEN NATHALIE CAME into Walter's room the following morning, it was to announce that on Fridays and Saturdays she had mid–day ballet classes and to ask if he'd mind driving her to the end of the subway line. No acknowledgement. No signs. Nothing. She just left and went downstairs.

It occurred to him that he was giving in to her all the time, and he began to feel resentful and wondered why he'd agreed. Yet, at the same time, he knew he could call up the startlingly powerful wave of pleasure, those central fiery pinpricks of pleasure which he seemed to be able to trigger like a conditioned rat simply by thinking about her face or repeating her name to himself. "Nathalie," he would say, and they would toboggan through his stomach like a soft explosion.

Then with a certain tenderness he thought of the moment of ejaculation, "The supreme moment of love–making," the sub–heading in the sex manual once read, "the intimate transfer of dna molecules." Never before had he quite appreciated that he was now being carried around, there where Nathalie worked in the kitchen, that those 'dna molecules' glistening between her legs in the bedroom light the night before had been in some measure an expression of himself, or that the speed and sureness with which she'd wiped them away on a tissue from under her pillow had made him that much the smaller person. Did it matter to her that he'd joined the club—he, Rutner, Kusiuski, all somehow absorbed into her life, footnotes in an amusing story? Walter stood motionless beside the shutters for several moments as the sunlight streamed across his naked thighs and Rutner's bees moved purposefully back and forth on their way to the hollyhocks beside the kitchen door. Then he heard Nathalie's impatient walk below suddenly approach the stairs.

"Walter? Walter, aren't you coming? I'm making you something to eat."

"Sorry! I'll be right down."

She looked up from the stove as he entered the kitchen.

"Well! Finally," she said, laughing. "What took you so long?"

"Just dressing."

She had greeted him so openly he went over to her and put his hand on her waist, but she just laughed and edged away. "No, no. You can't kiss me," she said hunching up her shoulders. "You'll eat off all my powder. Go sit at the table."

Walter did as he was told.

"Did you sleep well?"

"Oh, yes," he replied.

"I slept wonderfully, *wonderfully!* And now it's such a beautiful day, and I'm going to a *wonderful* ballet class, I could jump in the air, just like that. See? Did you like that?" She stood smiling in front of him, a little out of breath. "Ballet's so wonderful. It's so ecstatic. Don't you think so?"

Walter smiled wistfully and nodded, but he was sulky and didn't want to follow her in her enthusiasms.

"So," he said to her as he got up and went to sit down in Rutner's big rocking chair by the window. "Where do you think your next job will be?"

"Oh, I don't know. Something will turn up. It always does."

Walter stuffed his hands in his pockets and looked out over the garden.

"But what is it about it that you like so much?" he finally asked. "What do you get out of it?"

"What do I get out of what?"

"Ballet. The whole routine."

Nathalie looked at him with a kind of astonishment.

"Why, don't you understand, Walter? Ballet is life, resurrection! It's like being close to *god.* A ballet dancer suffers agony, *torture* just for such moments. Don't you understand that? Wonderful ecstatic moments when she can stand on one toe just that extra second longer. I hope that you don't think that you just get up there and stick your leg out." Nathalie raised hers. "No, no. You have to stretch, reach out, away from the earth, always away from the earth. See? You might think the muscles are relaxed, but of course they're not. They're pulling. See how hard?"

"You have to stretch, reach out, away from the earth...."

Walter saw the cords of her tendons lift beneath the skin.

"Georgi Virtanian is my teacher. He says you must be able to *kill* with your arches. Dance and cry, dance and cry, that's what ballerinas do. And do you know what else he says? He walks around the studio with a long stick and he says, 'Come on girls, suffer! Life is suffering! Dance is suffering! You must suffer to be beautiful!' And then he might take your leg and wrench it back against your shoulder, or hit you on the shins and say, 'Turn out, Nathalie! Turn out, for heaven's sake.' How wonderful it is!"

"It all sounds a little inhuman to me," Walter mused from his corner.

"Oh, humans, I hate them!" cried Nathalie. "Don't you know how beautiful statues are when they stand there? Or icons? Superb, beautiful icons?"

Walter smiled and nodded, but Nathalie was in her element. Didn't he know about Plesitskaia? Margot Fonteyne? Didn't he understand that if they ever gave up dancing, even at sixty, their muscles would knot up and it would be painful for them to walk after that? Didn't he understand sacrifice? Walter didn't say he found this difficult to accept—even to believe—and he just listened as she told him how she'd rush out to buy tickets for the best productions, the most expensive seats she could afford, in the front rows where she could see the dancers' muscles tremble, the expression on their faces, watch the hidden pressures of performance. Walter found all this rhapsodic, and he took it in with a mixture of envy and silent deprecation. Besides, she was trying to be like a nun, withdrawing and denying while she talked idly about how her face resembled some particular grace's in *La Primavera*. Worse, she pretended that her connections with the normal and the human were in some way forced, a violation of her spirit, and if this was her way of making him feel guilty for his secret demands on her, it worked. He fell into a morose, half-renunciatory state to appease her while she lapsed into a blank depression that he could neither understand nor do anything about. What had he done? She made him feel like a culprit as he drove her to the subway station later that morning, while she sat in the corner of the car and talked in a monotone about higher states of being and how she wished to return to a Bulgarian monastery she'd once visited on her travels, some place lost in the mountains like a medieval castle, predictably without electricity, and filled with a semi–punitive air of mysticism and orthodox rigour.

"How is it you don't understand these states?" she asked almost accusingly, tears welling up in her eyes and lending her face a reddened, spectral quality, almost frightening.

Walter looked at her, puzzled.

"Do you want to stay on the earth? Don't you want to be an angel?" She was almost pleading with him. "I always wanted a man who was like an angel! Don't you understand that? Like an angel!" and she had burst open the car door and fled down the walkway to the subway.

Walter was about to call out to her but for some reason thought better of it. He just sat there paralyzed, his hands gripping the steering wheel. Then he was about to get out of the car and run after her when he realized he was probably too late. Instead he just sat for a long time with his hands on the wheel, feeling humiliated, beaten, like a fly riding a pendulum. What had caused this sudden, inexplicable outburst? He didn't know. Had he said something? Done something? It occurred to him he might never see her again, and while he sat digesting that prospect, he began to wonder if he shouldn't just carry on down the road himself, west, because west was where he wanted to go, *The Champlain fur route*, god knew where to. And yet he made no move to get started, just stayed by the side of the road near the red and yellow subway sign, watching the people of the city come and go, as he thought about Rutner, the Polish boyfriend, himself, the intense feelings of sexual pleasure he could arouse simply by thinking of her face or pronouncing her name. He didn't understand her, he kept saying to himself, as though that by itself could resolve something. He just didn't understand her.

By the time he reached the highway he felt numbed. He stared in front of him as the white line stretched and curved beneath the wheels of his car, and just tried to assuage the beaten feeling that had overcome him. In an hour's time he found himself driving up the concession road that led to Helmut Rutner's farm. A dust-covered Japanese sportscar sat in the driveway, partially blocking the way and forcing him to park up on the grass. No one was in. The flies buzzed lazily about the kitchen window as the screen door closed behind him. Eleven thirty. Already it was hot. He checked upstairs and flopped onto the sepia couch. Another half–hour of day–dreaming depression, then he went to the window and looked out over the orchard. The trees shimmered in the wavering heat as though they were being baked to an essence. Through the glass he could almost smell the painful, semi–drugged fieldsmells like a fertile chloroform rising from below. And there where the pastures began, veiled and outfitted in white was Rutner, raising a frame from one of the hives while a host of furious insects circled about his head. He looked curiously at one with them, like a kind of chef, potting and stirring and mixing, while the maddened bees darted about him in wide arcs. Walter put on the hat, boots, and old labcoat Rutner had set aside for him the previous day and strode out to greet his friend.

Helmut hardly looked up as he arrived.

"Little bitches are as mad as hell in this heat," he said.

Calmly he brushed soft clusters of bees off the comb frames with a chicken feather while he instructed Walter to direct puffs of cedar smoke at them from an aluminum smoker. Still the bees would swoop angrily about Walter's body, and he was forced to carry each honey–laden frame quickly toward a tin–roofed cabin that housed some makeshift extracting equipment. As he ran, he shook the last of the bees from the frame or scraped at them with an old paintbrush. Then he would go back to the smoke and the buzzing for more.

"So where did you go this morning?" Helmut asked him as he put the roof back on a hive and covered it with a square stone.

"Oh, I took Nathalie to the end of the subway line."

Walter flicked a bee off his rubber boots. He felt sweaty and cramped, and he had decided to be taciturn. Rutner gave him an appraising glance, handed him an unused honey super, and motioned toward the tin–roofed shed.

"Bees are all dancers, you know that?" he said when Walter returned.

Walter looked up at him through his veil.

"Oh, yes, great dancers. Every little thing. Food supply, direction, all in the dance. Everything mathematical. Bred right into them, right from their cells. Precise, geometric. They see in hexagonal blocks, just like their comb. Fruitful thought, that. You see as you are." He scraped some dark, sticky substance from the top of the frame. "Then you build as you see," he added, almost as an afterthought.

Helmut deposited two empty supers beside the shed wall and opened the door. First he counted the honey–frames where Walter had leaned them one against the other beside a deep stainless steel tray. Then he set to work stripping the capping wax from the comb with an electrically heated knife. Slowly the dark liquid began to accumulate. Walter ran his finger through and tasted.

"Not bad, eh? Hundred and twenty pounds of honey in that hive." Helmut pointed to it swimming at the bottom of the tray. "You know what Virgil called that? Great poet, Virgil, but too fastidious. Spirit, he said. Pure spirit. Can you imagine a guy getting sucked in like that?"

"Sucked in like what?"

Helmut smiled and turned the frame around.

"I'll tell you one thing," he said, resting the end on the table. "One thing I learned from bees is not to get too impressed by their system. All that temptation for self-abandonment in there. Yessir. Bees'll teach you about that. You know drones can't see? Can't focus. Can't feed themselves. Can't fend off anybody because they don't have stingers. So come fall the old girls starve them, kick them out of the hive, let them loll around on the grass, then make new ones in the spring. Billions of generations all re–enforcing that kind of laxness and self–abandonment. Scary, man."

Helmut picked at a large piece of wax, popped it into his mouth, and motioned at Walter to do the same.

"Let me tell you another thing about drones. You know the old girls breed them for one purpose? One purpose, so they've got the biggest penises proportionate to size of anything in the animal kingdom—biggest bloody pokers. Use up so much energy getting it up they die after mating. No kidding. Not to mention the queen rips it out of their bodies while she's at it, just for good measure. Takes on three, five, maybe seven drones, saves up all the sperm in a little bag at the back. One time. Seven drones, good for the rest of her life—five, six years." He shook his head to himself. "That's the female system."

"What system?"

"The matriarchal system, man! All that honey. Ever see drones gobbling at it? Fat now, dead later. That's matriarchy! Set up shop as a goddess, initiate people, then rub them out. I figure that queen in there laying away carries around a little dark secret every woman's actually proud of."

"And what's that?"

"Death. They make it. Knit it all up like a little baby sock and gloat over it every night before they go to bed. That's matriarchy, man, I'm telling you."

Later that evening, as the small dark patches of moisture began appearing on the sides of the green sportscar, he and Walter were sitting on the verandah over mugs of honey sweetened tea. Helmut switched the topic of conversation back to Nathalie.

"I knew her really well, you know," he remarked, lolling impassively in his chair. "Really intimately. Even the birthmark at the top of her thigh. Little brown birthmark."

He looked to see whether Walter made any sign of recognition, but Walter gave none.

"I knew the whole taste of her. Bit like camembert. Sharp. Acidic sometimes. But—" He leaned back and exhaled a cloud of blue smoke. "Too intellectual. Passions too cerebral. Fractious girl. Skittish."

He seemed well pleased with the word as he canvassed Walter's face, and when he was satisfied with its effect he carried on.

"One thing I'll say about Nathalie, though. She was capable of real response sometimes. Surprise you with the intensity. Scare you almost. Really shake you up with what you could do."

Walter nodded drily.

"Howl like a little alley cat. Other times, nothing. Big overlay of neurasthenia. Lots of ideas, a lot of theories. Real victim of the hormones, if you know what I mean. Like a ten wheel truck. Get in gear, careen down a hill, all primed and oiled for one direction. You think you're riding along top of the world and then *bam!* Gears go haywire, big bloody grinding and clanking, you don't know what hit you. Ever seen how mad a bitch gets when the dogs go after her at the wrong time? Even if they *don't* go after her. Jesus! Watch out, man. I'm telling you."

Walter laughed despite himself.

"Nope. Real lack of simplicity there. I find I have to have that simplicity in a woman, smooth out the edges, leave breathing room for my imagination."

Helmut poured out two more cups of tea.

"You take Judy, now. You know her father's a big American industrialist?"

"Is that so?"

"Damn right. Bloody big industrialist, gives her everything she wants. But it hasn't really affected her. Still a really emotional girl. Really direct. No complications. A bit on the conventional side, maybe. That's always a problem for people like me. And her hands are a bit too big. Ever notice that? Big hands. Not quite the right proportion."

Walter raised his eyebrows and took to playing with his teaspoon.

"But at least she had the good sense not to get electrolysis done on her tits. Little bit of hair there, like the Greek girls. Natural. I really admire that in a woman."

ix

*F*ISH AND VISITORS *stink after three days.* Walter's
mother had taught him that one, and he'd begun to think
about it. Not that Helmut had said anything that morning.
He was going back to town. "To have a look at the proofs
for *Rasputin,*" he'd said, though more likely to visit Judy
Stoddard. He'd left Walter the keys almost ostentatiously,
as if to say Helmut Rutner was not one to mistrust his
houseguests or the first to be accused of being inhospi-
table. Besides, Walter had agreed to help him with some
chores. All things considered it was the least he could do.
And who could complain about moving some cases or putting a few empty honey frames in front of the hives to let
the bees clean up the last bits of honey on them? Nathalie
must have spent the night at her boyfriend's, Walter
concluded. Where else could she have gone? But without
her there, he'd begun to feel like an intruder, and he
thought Helmut must have sensed it too. He felt he ought
to leave soon, though he kept giving himself excuses not
to.

The first part of the morning he spent buying his friend groceries and laying out more money than he'd intended to in the process. He bought him cheese, salami, a lot of imported German beer. Then, after he'd made sure Allenby had fed the horse, he took a beer and lay down idly in the sun by the brook, thinking about Nathalie, calling up the soft toboggan explosion of pinpricks in his belly, pressing the cool brown bottle to his cheek, the myriad droplets already forming around it as though an essence pressed from its core. What could Helmut have meant by all that talk about drones and matriarchy? A wave of indefinable resentment passed over him. Why couldn't Rutner just say what he meant? And why had he been so pointed about having slept with her? When he thought of this, Walter felt suddenly confused and uncertain, as though the ground were sinking away beneath him. He had to put the beer down and shake his head. How strange the brook seemed to him at that moment, strange and perverse, a new brook he'd never seen before, but running from back in time, always the same water, the same little eddies and whirlpools, over black deep parts and shallow rocky parts, running before his eyes as it had before someone else's and would before someone else's again. He flicked away a mosquito that had landed on his arm and noticed the morning heat was acquiring an edge. Then, as he looked away from the sunlit sky, the name suddenly occurred to him. "Virtanian!" he said, almost aloud. The fact that he was able to remember made the final moments as he sipped the beer especially satisfying. In the drenching midsummer heat he walked slowly back to the house, the screen door clattering behind him.

"Virtanian!" He flipped through the pages of the telephone book.

Early that afternoon Walter was outside the ballet studio. He did not go in right away. Instead he preferred to watch the comings and goings along the street from inside the car, until he realized there might be a rear door and that he might miss her. Grey signs pointed up some stairs toward the sound of a piano. Near the top he noticed some orange peels, a fat silverfish scurrying into a crack. The piano had stopped, but he could hear the rhythmic scraping of feet across the floor. Then he peeped round the corner of the door. Bright, golden, the mid-day sun streamed through the windows, illuminating the dancers. As in a picture from Degas, the light washed over them as they moved in unison, some in pink, some in mauve, stretching and turning, filled with strength and grace. Walter was enchanted, more by this practice than by any performance, because it was like spying on the unknown, because it had the stamp of absolute reality, a *ne plus ultra*. The flesh tones, the freckles of redheads, the sprung curls, the thinness, even disproportion of some body torsos impressed themselves upon him not as some distant, got-up theatrical production, but as real, and yet raised, transfigured by the light that bathed them all and made them seem as one.

Still from his angle, he could not see if Nathalie was among them, and he was anxious not to stick his head too far round the corner lest he be told to leave.

"Now girils," came a voice from the front of the room. "I vant you pleas' do this. Pleas' in my class no talking. Pleas' everybody."

Walter heard the man's hands clap together, then "Madame!" and the pianist began to play again.

"Attitude, pliéh, relevéh, pirouette, arabesque. Pleas'."

The whole class began to move.

"*La*–tah, *la*–tah, *la*–tah–tah," said the voice. Then it stopped.

"Everybody! I vill explain something to you. In a'Russia, in Bolshoi ballettc, vc do pirouette this vay."

Walter heard a scrunching on the floor.

"Here you do it this vay. Now ve do correct *classical* vay."

The music began again. Walter peeked more boldly round the door and caught a glimpse of a nervous, balding man with his hair combed from somewhere over his left ear all the way across his scalp, the glint of a single Soviet–style gold tooth as he spoke.

"Breav'," he was saying. "Breav', always breav'. Ven you do attitude, ven you do relevéh, pleas' breav' from very deep in the lungs. You look longer, lighter. And girils, pleas'. Not like dogs in trees. *La*–tah, *la*–tah, *la*–tah–tah. Von, two, tree, four. Feet pleas' not like hooks. Very good! But pleas', pleas' girils, feeling! I hate formalizm! I hate formalizm in class!"

He shouted these words again as he walked out. Immediately he caught sight of Walter.

"Ah! Come in my office pleas'."

Walter hesitated and looked into the classroom to see if Nathalie was still there.

"Come in my office, pleas'," the man repeated per-emptorily as he walked briskly down the hall.

Walter followed him in.

"Sit down, sit down, pleas'," he said, looking him straight in the eye. "I have been thinking about you, and I think ve must put you in intermediary 2, becaus' this class is better for you becaus' you need jumping, jump, jump— very important for boys. But you must come every day. Very important to—"

Before he could say any more, a thirtyish woman who had caught the gist of their conversation sidled over to him.

"Georgi!" she said, with an annoyed frown. She whispered something into his ear.

"Oh, I am so sorry!" he suddenly grinned. "Vy don't you say something? You are just like a student ve have, yes just like a boy. I am so sorry. Excus' me pleas'."

He got up and left. Walter smiled a silly smile to the woman and shrugged. Then he saw Nathalie walking down the hall towards the stairs. He jumped out of his seat.

"Walter!" she cried as soon as she caught sight of him. "What are you doing here?"

"Oh, I came to see how you were. I hope you don't mind."

"Of course I don't mind. You can come and have coffee with me and then you can drive me to Casik's place, alright?"

The first part of the proposal suited Walter just fine. The second completely baffled him.

"I was kind of hoping he'd been declared dead," he finally ventured.

"Oh, Walter. You don't understand things, do you. It's true. I did declare him dead. But Casik is a wonderful man, don't you see? He's helped me a very great deal."

She put emphasis on this. Walter would have to judge just how much *a very great deal* was. Power enough to resurrect, at least, he thought to himself.

"Now I see we're having our difficulties over these things. Well, I'm going to tell you about Casimir Kusiuski, alright? Do you want to hear?"

Walter was diffident.

"Well, do you?"

x

AND SO OVER VIENNESE COFFEE, *mit schlag,* naturally *mit schlag,* and small mocha cakes, Walter Taylor finally got to hear about Nathalie Doroshkov's Polish boyfriend, not that he particularly wanted to, or if he did, it was to a tale far less flattering than what he was treated to. Ten years before it seemed, Kusiuski had left Poland with his Czech wife, Katerina, a would–be model who hated France where they'd first settled and who later returned to her native country. The beautiful Katerina had dumped him: Kusiuski was guilt–ridden, too Catholic. According to Nathalie he had never forgotten her, and after a stint in Chicago and a brief marriage to a German girl called Margite, he'd moved to Canada where he now sustained himself on the modest but growing reputation of books he'd published in France on the structure of a pair of medieval texts. And when to all this Nathalie added a charming testimonial to his *extraordinary* kindness, the Swiss chocolate bars he would buy for her, the midnight rides they would take in his Volvo whenever she got depressed, Walter's misgivings had only grown worse. Kusiuski was magnanimous. Kusiuski was established. Kusiuski was, as Nathalie had said herself, *experimenté*. Walter was downcast. She had drawn a picture of a spare, frosty–eyed forty year old, filled with vigour and success and with a list of accomplishments that seemed like a wallet full of credit cards. And yet she didn't live with him *on a full time basis*. Walter wondered if that were meant as a tribute to her independence. She didn't believe in people sticking to each other like glue. She wasn't his third wife, and besides there was her work. What did he think? She was a parasite?

Later Walter was nervous, already morose, and as he drove her through downtown streets lined with cobblestones, with the mess of poles and streetcar wires overhead, he could see on either side the dark, deep-verandahed houses. Out front sycamore and horse chestnut trees almost reached in toward the darkness. Why had he come here, he would ask himself as he looked out over the hood of the car. But when he stole sidelong glances at her, he knew why, and he would feel confused, overwhelmed by longing and uncertainty.

First the streetcar wires, then the fashionable reclamation work, sandblasted brick, and releaded stained glass of one of the more house–proud areas of the city, comfortable, restored, faintly meretricious, where Nathalie cried, "Here! Stop!" just as Walter was about to pass a tiny courtyard filled with brick shalings and enclosed by a low wrought iron fence. On the front door of the house stood a substantial looking brass knocker.

"Zsoozshko!" she cried as the door opened. "There you are!"

She set her black bag at his feet and quickly embraced him. Kusiuski smiled and mumbled something inaudible.

"Ah ha! What's this?"

Knocking his glasses askew in the process, she dived playfully into his shirt pocket and extracted a little checkered piece of paper.

"Oh, sorry darling. I'm sorry. Did I hurt you?"

Casimir Kusiuski looked a little foolish and dishevelled.

"No, no," he smiled amicably. "It's quite alright. Just a—a little chess game I played and didn't do very well in."

"Oh, poor baby."

She shifted the paper into his jacket pocket and looked towards Walter.

"Now Casimir! Here you must meet Walter Taylor who brought me."

"Yes, yes of course. You are the young man who drove—"

Walter was nodding agreeably.

"From Ottawa," he said.

"From Ottawa. Good! Good! Well, come in. Do come in."

Kusiuski smoothed his hair and extended his hand. It was white, plump, and very finely manicured. In fact as Walter quickly grew accustomed to the paler light in the vestibule, he realized most of Kusiuski was just that. His prominent teeth revealed themselves in a kindly, well–fed smile. His face, flattish and weakly contoured, vaguely resembled a rabbit's. But he was tall, remarkably tall at

6'4". Three large gold rings spread themselves evenly across the fingers of his left hand, and on his feet he wore little leather slippers. Kusiuski ushered him into the living room.

"Sit down. Sit down. Can I get you something? Brandy? Martini?"

Walter shuffled his feet a little.

"Oh, just a little wine, please."

Kusiuski disappeared a moment.

"What was she doing with him?" he wondered. He shook his head to himself.

From what he could make out, most of Kusiuski's house was painted entirely in white, sparsely furnished: leather, glass, stainless steel, a few plants. Toward the front of the living room there sat what appeared to be a dull white plastic box with a scattering of pastel coloured journals on it, a modish, chrome–plated chess set, over-sized, and a decorative nonsense machine encased in glass. Three metal balls issued from an opening at the top, rolled down a chute, leapt over a few little interstices, and finally dropped somewhere into a hole at the bottom only to reappear again. Walter watched it for a moment.

"It's a bit amusing, no?" Casimir smiled indulgently at him as he handed him a glass. "A friend of mine used to make them in New York, but they never sold too well here. I rather like it."

"Yes, it's interesting," said Walter.

"So," Kusiuski said as he settled into a chair. "Nathalie tells me you have been staying with Helmut Rutner for a while."

"Oh, yes."

[105]

"And how is—what is it? Ah, yes! How is *Rasputin* coming?"

Walter smiled.

"Quite well, I think. He seems to have it all ready. He read it the other night. Maybe Nathalie mentioned it to you."

"Yes, I think she did mention something. By the way," he said, craning his neck backwards. "Where did she go?"

"I'm in here, Casik! I'll be out in a moment. I'm just getting changed."

"Ah. And what about you? Where was it you said you were off to...?"

"Oh, west for the summer, I thought. I've never been."

"West, of course. Yes. The land of the native. Very popular these days."

"Pardon me?"

"Oh, nothing. It's just the west as distinct from the *European*. You see what I'm getting at. The land of the savage. Or as Nietzsche would have it, the world of delight born of pain. Excuse a few intellectual remarks. You know what it's touted as, of course. The saviour. Not only that, the *indigenous* saviour. I don't mean you personally, of course, and yet I find nothing more absurd. Freud discovered the west and he called it the id. No? Shakespeare had his Caliban, Conrad his Congo.... I won't bore you. It's just that this west is a cobweb spun out by a spider who lives on the other side of the Atlantic, I believe. A very amusing fellow, I'm sure. Even urbane. Perhaps he has even taken up residence in Toronto. We can only hope temporarily."

As Walter made no reply, Kusiuski felt free to continue.

"You know," he said, settling back, "speaking of joy in pain, I was in Chicago last week for a series of conferences and I heard a most interesting monograph. Are you familiar at all with the works of Sacher-Masoch?"

Walter shook his head.

"Well, neither was I, frankly. But did you know he was Galician?" For some reason Kusiuski was pleased with this news. "Yes! An historian by training, it seems, apparently fascinated by the problems of polyglot kingdoms."

He took a sip of his drink.

"But it was his solution to the Slavic question I found so remarkable. Some frightful tsarina, I believe, complete with furs and whip. They were to be beaten into shape, I suppose."

He laughed.

"More savagery! And these terrible tsarina figures are always at the thick of it, don't you find?"

Walter shrugged and smiled as he glanced down at the chessboard.

"Do you play by any chance?" Kusiuski asked.

"A little."

"Splendid! I'm an addict myself. Can't keep away from it. We must have a game.... So. And how is Rutner these days?"

"Very well, I think. I don't know him that well, but I—I guess he's enjoying himself."

"Mmm."

Kusiuski adjusted himself confidentially in his seat.

"He is a strange one, you know. He wanted me to take him partridge hunting up north last summer. Nathalie may have told you I own a small island up there. God knows why I bought it. I'm not one for exercise of that sort. To tell you honestly if I could have my way, I would just as soon dispense with moving around altogether. Walking, lawncutting—" He swept them all away with his hand. "But I'll be damned if he didn't persuade me! He got up there—Nathalie was with us—and, well, he paddled that canoe like an expert, bagged six of those birds, grabbed them where they lay flapping, and wrung their necks just like that. Just like that! Really. It was amazing. He said it was the first time he had shot anything larger than a robin. Is it possible do you think? And so proficient! —Ah, *ptashe,* there you are."

Nathalie had just entered the room and sat down opposite Walter. She was wearing another pair of black pants and a linen chemise, brilliantly embroidered in dark silk.

"I was just telling Walter here about Helmut Rutner's attempt to get me away from my philosopher's chair."

Nathalie gave him a peculiar smile.

"Well, perhaps he should try again. You might not need your bag of yeast in the cupboard." She turned gaily toward Walter. "Do you know he has a big bag of yeast in the kitchen cupboard? He thinks it will help him *au boudoir.*" She laughed mischievously, then looked toward Kusiuski. "Does Margite still use that chalet?" she asked, à propos of nothing.

Kusiuski flushed a little and turned away.

"Oh–h, Zsoozshko's grumpy," she said, still smiling.

But Kusiuski remained in his seat, his large face smitten with some nameless offence.

"Don't be mad," she said lightly. Then a little agitated herself, she rose from her seat. "Maybe Walter, you would like to see the room Casik had built for me?" She glanced at Kusiuski, then motioned across the hall.

She led him to a large, airy room that had once been used as a kind of salon, though she explained nothing about the little incident that had just occurred or why she'd felt compelled to take him away. He looked carefully about him. A bed stood in a window alcove decorated with a profusion of potted plants. The hardwood floors had been left unsanded. On the wall opposite him hung a full rank of mirrors. The other a ballet bar bisected, running half the length of the room like a misplaced bannister. This was where she practised then, he thought to himself. He wondered about Kusiuski in the other room and glanced back over his shoulder, half expecting him to have followed them in, but there was no one there.

"Well," he said, mustering his social manners as he walked over to the window and peeped out at the view. "So this is where you live!"

"Yes. Sometimes. I don't live here all the time, you know."

"Oh?" Walter turned from the view. "Where else do you live?"

"What do you think? I've got jobs to take. I go to Europe. I stay with my parents. Why should I stay here all the time?"

Walter shrugged then turned to examine a collection

of little music boxes Nathalie had lined up on a shelf. She seemed unusually brisk and pre–occupied.

"Besides, sometimes I get to hate all this junk here. All this clutter, drawings, abstract paintings, eternal Bach. And books! God, what do I hate more than to be cooped up in a room filled with them. So many blabbermouths." She motioned toward the door. "Do you know he loves his books so much he wouldn't have the movers touch them when he came here? No, I swear, he and his friend Victor put every book into two satchels each—you know the schoolboys' bags? And they brought them here in a car. Forty trips they must have made, the two of them. Can you imagine? Isn't that priceless? And all for his wretched, wretched culture. It's all so spiteful, don't you think?"

Nathalie brushed vigorously at some creases in a pair of pants, smoothed out her bedspread, then walked over and stood beside him.

"Would you like to see how that works?"

She took the music box from his hands, pressed something at the rear, and opened the lid. Three little ballerinas in ivory began to whirl away round a mirror–like disk.

"Isn't that wonderful?" she said, relaxing a little. "This one's my favourite, of course, but I have an old antique one too. Casik bought it for me. Here, would you like to see it? It needs records, though."

She took some bronze plates from faded paper jackets and set one on the machine. It was round and punched, like a metal computer card.

"Fascinating," said Walter, holding the lid. As the music stopped, he looked up at her.

"Don't mind me," she said. "I feel a little ill."

Kusiuski made his appearance a few moments later and invited Walter to have a game of chess with him. He seemed jocular, well–disposed, as though he'd made a resolution to forget the little incident of the moment before and was determined to succeed. Walter, however, wasn't keen. All he really wanted to do was leave. Not so much to go back to Rutner's. That would have seemed too much like a defeat. More perhaps just to listen to the children playing or to the last sounds of the birds at dusk, and generally to feel older and superfluous and a little sorry for himself. He'd stayed too long. He wished Kusiuski had been more of an idiot, but he played, absently at first, trying to think of how he could get to see Nathalie again, and then under pressure, with a growing involvement.

Kusiuski, for his part, was very sure of himself, eccentric to a degree, single–minded, knowledgeable. He pressed his attack down the flanks, abandoned the centre and avoided castling, deflecting Walter's tentative threats and throwing him quickly on the defensive. Walter played tensely, expecting defeat, upset by the odd size and shape of the pieces, his hand noticeably shaking as he lifted the men, something he could do nothing to hide. His orthodox game stood him in poor stead. After only a dozen moves, he castled into an onslaught of pawns, was forced into a poor exchange, and was rescued only by Nathalie bringing in a large tray of coffee. He felt sheepish and embarrassed. Kusiuski, on the other hand, was expansive.

"Ah, coffee!"

He took the cup Nathalie had poured for him, blew across the surface, and pressed it gently to his lips as she excused herself and pointed toward her room.

"You know," he said, as he sat back from the board, "in chess there are really two games that can be played—the psychological game and the technical game. Wouldn't you agree? And I must confess my preference is for the second. So much cleaner, clearer. Just the lamp and the chess–board, the basic essentials, without that super–charged rococo tournament atmosphere. No one thumping his pieces down as though every move was a defence of one's ego. No histrionics. Just the deep structure of the game, the inner structure—that is where the real interest of the game lies.

"Of course in my younger days I used to play competitively—nothing exceptional, mind you, just for the sport of it. And I can remember myself, my reaction. Why the pieces coming at me were almost frightening in their potency. They had a kind of weight to them. Rooks pushing forward. Maddeningly positioned knights. The advanced pawn like the point of a chisel. I swear they were like extensions of my opponent's private will, almost organic, invading me, undermining me, reducing my scope. A mate was almost the annihilation of my being, profoundly upsetting. There was nothing I could do, and naturally I hated to resign. Loathed it. I was under someone's control, like a victim digested by a snake, and I'm not sure if I didn't enjoy my writhing, perversely of course. Do you follow me?"

Walter nodded politely, but he looked away. Why did everything Kusiuski say seem like some sort of parable to him? He didn't know, but suddenly he began to feel himself judged without being able to say why. He felt his smile begin to tense on his face.

"And you know," Kusiuski continued, "I think some-times of what Spassky has said. That when the game is over he actually physically misses his opponent, *needs* him, win or lose, wishes him back again. Or the great Nimzovitch—a master technician—forced to resign by an inferior player. Do you know what he did? You know he danced around in a rage on the top of the tables, practically tearing out his hair, yelling 'Why must I lose to this idiot?' Now *that* is what I mean by the psychological element, the completely expendable psychological element."

Kusiuski sipped again at his coffee, absorbed by his own train of thought.

"Mind you, it took me years to understand the situation objectively. How all was a simple collection of lines of force, the manipulation of vectors. And I began to delight in the geometry of the thing, the purely formal element, totally impersonal. What a liberation! What a breath of fresh air! No more dark, egotistical struggles. No Gothic extinctions, no more titanic flim flam and psychic machinations. Just purity of line, compositional technique. Do you know how much more reassuring this sort of approach is? Almost by itself it solves problems. Wouldn't you agree."

Walter was agreeing. Walter would have agreed to anything. Why had he come here, he asked himself again, knowing full well the answer. This was always the result of intruding! Why couldn't he learn that? He was about to return to his losing position when Nathalie Doroshkov entered the living room with her hair done up and a bag on her arm.

"Zsoozshko! Why didn't you tell me sooner about that phone message?"

Kusiuski looked up.

"The phone message? Ah! I don't know, *ptashe*. It must have slipped my mind."

"Don't you realize they want me to go to New York? In the *corps de ballet?* I get to go to New York for six weeks! Walter, isn't that wonderful? Oh, my god, Casik. I'm so excited. I *mustn't* miss my toe–class."

"But darling, you just came from a class."

"I've *got* to go, Casik. It's too important!"

Walter rose from his chair.

"Actually, I think I'd better be—"

"You don't have to go just because I'm going, you know," Nathalie said smiling at him.

"Oh, no, no. I've got some relatives here I should see, so...."

"Too bad," Casik remarked. "Too bad. We must finish another time."

"I'm sorry," Nathalie declared, impatiently. "I'm *terribly* late. Thank you for driving me, Walter," she called back through the doorway. "I hope I'll see you again! Good–bye. Good–bye, Casik!"

Moments later Walter left, awkward, mute, feeling as though he'd been physically beaten. He walked past the brick shalings, past the wrought iron fence, across the street and into the little parked car piled with apples and pipe tobacco. He turned on the ignition, left the motor running for a moment, and stared blankly through the windshield. Like an incantation, the ballet master's words circled round and round in his head: "Breav', breav', always breav'. It makes you look longer, lighter."

And she wanted a man like an angel. *Like an angel!* Resurrection, she had said. And there she was with Kusiuski, with chess pieces and music boxes, Swiss chocolate bars and midnight rides in Volvos, portly balding Kusiuski who needed his yeast bag *au boudoir*. Walter couldn't understand it, and a wave of bitter resentment passed over him. "Why do you want to stay on the earth?" she had asked him. Yet Rutner seemed the very incarnation of the earth, earthy Rutner, as Kusiuski was the incarnation of his machines. He remembered the muddy path to the stream, chewed with hoofmarks, the rutted animal track, and he almost hated her.

"Breav', breav', always breav'."

And yet how beautifully she had stood there in her mauve tights, the tight golden curls, the sunlight streaming through the third storey windows, as elegant and graceful and beautiful as her limbs that rose in unison with the others. "Higher, higher, closer to god," he heard her saying, and for that brief moment she had succeeded, he was sure. To himself he would say "Nathalie," and the soft tobogganing explosions of pinpricks in his belly moved like a sheet of pleasure across his body, like a confirmation.

xi

IN HIS CALMER MOMENTS, as he drove back in the car, Walter would think to himself how some people were like air. They moved about from flower to flower, unaffected by things. Other people were heavy. Life washed over them, and they absorbed it and absorbed it, until they couldn't absorb any more. Maybe he was one of the heavy ones, he would think, like the drones Rutner had warned him about. He could never have just picked up and left the way Nathalie had, for example, New York or no New York. Just like that! How was it she made no connection to anything? For an instant he wondered if she might have had the same effect on Kusiuski as she did on him, but that thought was quickly superseded by the prospect of facing Helmut Rutner. If he knew, he'd judge him for sure in his lecturing way. Already Walter was determined to keep what had happened to himself.

Yet he felt somehow resentful and searched round for ways to defend himself from Rutner's nameless accusations. At other moments, he would call to mind the intense visual impression of Nathalie's body, even to so minute a degree as the lie of the hair across her forearm, and that too would be superseded by an overwhelming feeling of helplessness that left him so enraged he found, to his amazement, he'd pushed the speedometer of his car past 80 miles and hour, the little engine grinding as it reached its limits.

He was flushed and sweating when he arrived. Once again, Rutner wasn't in, but this time Walter looked out over the bee–yard straightaway. There was no serene potting and mixing. He could see Helmut dashing about, lifting frames of honey and rushing toward a shed closer to the house, then back again. Walter ran downstairs, forgetting even his makeshift equipment.

"Get them out of here!" Rutner yelled as soon as Walter showed up.

"What?"

"Here! Take them to the shed near the house!"

He thrust a honey frame into Walter's hands.

"What about the bees on them?"

"Shake them off! Blow on them. Use the paint brush. Just get them out of here!"

Walter had no veil, no coat, no gloves, none of the things he needed to protect himself. And now, bareheaded, he ran toward the house, trying to outdistance the bees who'd been knocked off the frame, and at the same time trying to blow hard enough to get rid of the little round butt-end of bees still gorging themselves on honey in the comb. He had to poke at them with the bristles of a brush,

[117]

three or four in odd corners, and they emerged furious, darting, skimming. One dived at his shirt. He swatted it and went back for another frame.

Ten yards away from the extracting shed, he realized what had happened. He'd left the door open. Despite all his good intentions that morning, he'd left the door open, and two dozen frames of unripened honey had been enough to provoke bedlam. Hundreds of bees had converged on the shed. Now they were wrestling each other, darting crazily about, stinging one another to death. A litter of dead or dying bees lay across the floor, Rutner at the center of them.

"Make it fast, man! Only two left!"

A cloud of bees raced about Walter's head. Three quarters of the way back to the house he felt a buzzing and a burrowing at his hair, reached up with his free hand, and almost staggered under the sudden jolt of venom.

"Jesus!"

"Don't stop!"

Rutner raced by with the last frame in his own hands. Walter picked up the one he'd dropped and carried on, but when he finally sat down at the back stairs, a hot wave seemed to seep down from the top of his head. His eyesight wavered slightly.

"Here. Let me take a look."

Rutner parted the hair on his head, then with a flicking motion of his thumb, scraped something clear from his scalp.

"Vicious bitches. You don't want to leave the stinger in there or it'll be worse. There. You o.k.?"

Walter nodded and Helmut returned to the extracting

shed, closed the door, and draped a large canvas tarpaulin over the front. Then he went into the kitchen to make tea while Walter tried to recover. Rutner had his large curved pipe clouding the air of the verandah when he came back, just as the first evening stars appeared. Walter sipped at his tea, morose, uncommunicative, the swelling on his scalp tender and inflamed.

"You go into the city today?" Rutner finally asked.

"For a bit."

"See Nathalie?"

Walter looked up at him. Rutner seemed very proud of his guesses.

"Briefly. She had a lot to do."

"Mmm," Helmut said and gazed briefly up toward the darkening sky. Some sententiousness was building in him, Walter felt sure. He was beginning to recognize the signs: the pursed lips, the jaunty, questioning attitude of the head, the air of abstraction.

"You know," Rutner began, in his most annoying, principled tone, "One thing I learned working here is you can't be irresponsible. Practical life—I have great respect for practical life. It teaches you that. Disciplined passions, attention to detail. A lot of people told me about that, but only working here did I really get to know what it meant. Practical life's a great measure of a man, you know that? Greatest yardstick. Is he awake, right on top of things, or not? Can he get the job done, or is he suffering from *delirium praecox?* 'Classicism is health; romanticism is disease.' Goethe said that, you know. Great man, Goethe. I remind myself of that every now and again. Keeps me from getting too self–absorbed, losing perspective."

Walter said nothing in return, could say nothing as the pain jabbed itself down from the top of his skull. For a while Rutner smoked in silence on the verandah until the mosquitoes started to pester and land.

"Look, I'm sorry about the bees," Walter finally muttered. He felt irritated, trapped. *Delirium praecox?* What the hell did Rutner mean by *delirium praecox?*

"Forget it, man. It's alright. Don't worry about it." Then, after a pause, Helmut added. "Look, Judy'll need some help painting her apartment tomorrow, if you're up to it. Maybe you could give us a hand."

Walter nodded curtly and went inside.

Later that night, alone in the bed that was ultimately Rutner's bed, where what seemed like an æon ago Nathalie Doroshkov had lain, had smiled and talked, Walter Taylor searched for a place on the pillow to rest his swollen head and wondered what on earth had made him agree to go to Judy Stoddard's the following morning. Guilt? Did he feel he had to pay Rutner back for the bees he'd cost him? In any event, he'd let Helmut's lecturing bother him more than the bees, and he was mad at himself for not answering back. Practical life! He'd seen enough of Rutner's practical life to have much respect—the tea–stained mess in the kitchen, the yellowed, spindly house plants, the washer so filled with dirty clothes it stank. Besides, it was Allenby who looked after the cattle, pastured them, milked them. Walter had caught sight of him often enough skulking about early in the mornings, trying to be inconspicuous the way people do when they run a place and don't think they should. So that was practical life? It made him sick.

In the car the next morning, dressed in the old clothes Rutner had lent him, Walter felt gawky and uncomfortable. The top of his head still throbbed. He was still sullen, uncommunicative, and this time Rutner reciprocated in kind. Nor did the mood improve much when they reached the old sub–divided houses of Judy Stoddard's part of town. She greeted them from the top of the stairs, the red bandana in her hair lending a special glow to her fresh, freckled face. All of a sudden she was living intensely. Two young men at her service. Plus she had just helped her first struggling artist by buying a painting. It was called *The Tomb of Reason,* and she had it propped up in her hallway beside some paint cans and a roller tray.

"Who did it?" Helmut asked.

"Oh, the fellow who lives upstairs."

"Is that so?"

Some dotted lines fanned out from the corner of a sheet of graph paper. In the lower half sat a cellophane bag filled with human hair around which were pencilled a number of tiny equations, runes, such as $E = $ Apollo / *et cetera.*

Helmut turned up his nose.

"You should meet him, you two, really," said Judy. "He lives with his wife who's very pregnant, an American girl I think and—" She looked behind her in mock conspiracy. "—I think with his mistress as well."

"Really?" said Walter.

"Yes! She's always up there whenever Maria's gone to work, and the two of them always look as though they've just fallen out of bed. I don't know how Maria puts up with her."

Helmut muttered something incomprehensible. Then he made a few remarks about modern decadence. There was something sacred between a man and a woman, a physical rhythm, delicate, mysterious, easy to break. Then he started criticizing the rotten intellectualism of the painting she'd just bought. Too many straight lines, willful, neurotic.

"Not enough woman's ass in this painting," he declared, running his hand down Judy's back. "See how beautiful a woman's ass is?" he added appraisingly for Walter's benefit. "God damn beautiful!"

"I have the paint here," Judy said quickly. "And I bought some tint to put into it if we need to, but I'm really not sure of the colour."

But Helmut was grumpy. She had deflected him from his tirade against philandering and phoney liberalism, and he took it out on her by declaring the colour co-ordinated life vacant, unspiritual, and not of the essence. He wasn't fussy about the *Better Homes and Gardens* approach. Practicality. Clean, fast work. That was the main thing. Nor was he going to waste time getting down to it. He divided up the work between them. Judy would wash the walls. He would paint them, and Walter found himself in the role of Helmut's assistant. That was bad enough, but Helmut had decided to become pontifical, and it wasn't long before Walter began to chafe and fume.

"See this?" Helmut said, dancing Walter's brush heavily into the corners of the woodwork. "Too much and you splay the bristles."

Moments later he took the top of a paint can and studiously poured paint into it. Then he took a small brush and filled it.

"That's the secret to window–dressing," he declared. "Lots of paint on the brush." He was something of a professional, he explained for Judy's benefit. That's how he'd got through university.

"Use the roller on the big surfaces," he'd call out when he saw Walter struggling with a heavy four–inch brush.

But Walter ignored him.

"Look," Helmut said five minutes later as he came by to inspect the work. "I told you to use the roller on the big surfaces. It goes faster."

"I don't mind the brush," said Walter.

"Suit yourself," said Helmut.

Walter didn't answer. Instead he simply pursed his lips and rankled at the extra flourishes Helmut began to add to his roller just to make it obvious how superior his workmanship really was. Walter held doggedly to his brush. Later, when he caught a glimpse of him necking briefly with Judy, his hand on her breast, he wondered if there were some special mechanism in women that blinded them to Rutner's sort of bullying. "God, what an idiot!" he declared. But it was a scene that pre–occupied him. Painting a small pantry off the kitchen, free from the latent oppression of being in the same room with him, Walter pondered the problem.

There must have been something the matter with her if she didn't see what was going on. He knew Rutner's attitude toward her. Her hands were too big. That's what he'd said. She was conventional. He'd said that too. What did she need that for? Especially somebody like her. She seemed nice enough, after all, still with a kind of freshness to her, not like Rutner's sallow puffiness. Compassionate, disappointed, mildly philosophical, Walter soon found himself shaking his head at the little scene he'd just witnessed. What could he do? People were like that. He began to take a certain solace from his work. He spread his quart of white enamel over the pantry's baseboards and door frames, hiding strands of old bell–wire, letting the paint drip gently into crevices where Judy's scrub brush had failed to reach and managing for his efforts to feel at least partially relieved.

Afterwards Rutner became very charming with Judy. He praised the salad she had made. He put a bit of dressing on the tip of his tongue and clucked knowledgeably. "That's really good," he said, squinting, but she had forgotten one thing, a few bottles of beer. Did she mind? He could get them in a jiffy. As for Walter, of course, Helmut's sudden departure was a positive relief. He breathed more easily. The paint seemed to flow better. And after a few moments of work Judy came and stood in the doorway of the pantry.

"I just realized I haven't had a chance to thank you," she began.

"For what?"

"Why, for all this!" she replied and motioned about the room. "It's a wonderful job!"

"Oh, not that much, really."

"Nonsense. I know how much work it is. I'm really very pleased." She smiled at him. "You were at Helmut's reading that night, weren't you?" she asked as she sat down on a low stool.

"Yes I was."

"And how did you enjoy it?"

"Oh, quite well, I suppose. It was—well, it was interesting."

There was a pause. He hesitated, looked up at her again, then went back to his brush. "Actually, though, I think I've been having some second thoughts about it."

"Oh? Why?"

"Well, I don't know. Rasputin. The general directions of it. It all seemed a little disturbing."

"Disturbing?"

"Yes. Violent." He'd said this with more emphasis than he'd at first intended.

"You know," she replied musingly, "That's interesting you should say that. I've always found my father was a violent sort of man."

Walter didn't quite see the connection, but she was very earnest and he was touched.

"Really?"

"Not like Rasputin, but yes, I think the war made my father violent. It's always been something I disliked, violence."

Walter nodded solemnly. He sat for a moment waiting for her to resume the conversation, but she didn't.

"I suppose in his field he's got to keep his head above water," he finally remarked.

"What do you mean?"

"Well, Helmut mentioned that your father was some kind of industrialist...."

Judy laughed.

"Is that what he said?"

"Yes he did."

"Well, he's not an industrialist. He's an insurance executive."

"Oh."

Judy suddenly came closer to him.

"Walter, do you know you have paint all over your hair? Let me get you some turpentine."

She had got Walter to sit down on the stool when there was a rattling at the door. Helmut Rutner had returned. He gave the two of them a quick glance and sidled over to examine the problem.

"You'll probably have to cut that patch out," he finally said.

"What do you mean?" asked Judy.

"Well, he's got that bee–sting there and that stuff's hard to get out sometimes, that's all. It really sticks."

Walter took the rag from Judy's hand. "It's alright," he said. "I'll work on it." Then he went to the bathroom and closed the door.

xii

THEY PAINTED WELL into the evening in an atmosphere of restraint and mutual suspicion that made
concentration on his work the most practical way to
escape. Whenever he noticed Helmut grab Judy or run his
hand down the back of her jeans, he assumed Rutner was
doing it partly for his benefit, and he became so much the
more frustrated and irritable. For his part Helmut was
displeased when Judy wouldn't agree to let him stay the
night with her and insisted on going to her girlfriend's.

"Look, Judy," he had said, "I can't drive in and help
you paint tomorrow because I've got to see Jackson about
the final proofs for *Rasputin* tomorrow morning at eleven.
If we stay we can get it done before that. What's a little
paint, anyway? We can open the windows."

"No! Paint fumes are dangerous, Helmut. I'll manage
tomorrow, that's all."

Helmut retaliated by deciding that he needed a rest,
one which began to bear all the earmarks of a sit–down

strike. He pulled out a small pocket Thesaurus and insisted he found it necessary to spend fifteen minutes every night sharpening his vocabulary.

"You lose a lot of words if you don't keep coming across them," he said. "Take *pertinacious*. Isn't that a great word? Maybe it's the sound: pert. A pert word. A bit impertinent. Or *perfunctory*. Maybe it's the 'func' sound. Func. Like flunky."

The atmosphere as he and Walter drove home in the car that evening was no better, and Rutner didn't improve things when he began an expansive lecture on the evils of obstinacy in women. It had to be checked. Not only did it lead to the gradual enfeeblement of the male, undermining him and sapping his confidence, but it encouraged the crowd of duplicitous men who were always around ready to cash in on disharmony between the sexes. You had to be skeptical. Like old Ovid said, the husband never had to worry about his enemies, since it was his best friends who caused all the trouble.

And by the time they'd got back to the farm, Helmut was on to Picasso. He had a penchant for great artists. He liked to draw parallels.

"You know what he said? Great master, Picasso. He said all women are either goddesses or doormats. That's it, man. Sixty years old, the guy gets himself a beautiful woman, sensitive, forty years younger than he is. Then he starts wiping his feet all over her. Threatens to throw her into the Seine. Tells her she has to devote herself to him. Cuts her right off from her family—clean break. And when she starts getting uppity, he gets her pregnant. Bang! Two kids."

Walter listened to this sullenly.

"All that seems rather brutal to me," he stated, after a pause.

Helmut shook his head. He hadn't quite expected opposition.

"These days you can't afford to be sentimental, man. You've got to have an ego like that sometimes. Too many forces to contend with, trying to distract your energy."

Walter looked resolutely at the floor.

"I'll tell you one thing, though," Helmut added. "Maybe you can make a goddess into a doormat, but it doesn't work the other way around. That's Judy's trouble, you know that? Too domestic. No sacred fire. A good woman's got to be an accomplice, the two of you, stealing fire. But Judy? Placid. Too placid. Mind you, I'm a great believer in the maternal instinct. But you need that sneaking accomplice part, the fiery soul. It bothers me, Judy's background. I don't know if she can stand the test of living with me. They all want to live with artists, these bourgeois girls—put some meaning into their lives, but.... Still, lots of money there, man. Big bloody American industrialist for a father? Jesus! It's good to have the cash mattress around like that sometimes, you know, in case they push you on your ass too much."

"I don't know if I agree with that kind of approach," said Walter after a minute. "It just seems like more chauvinism to me."

Helmut Rutner was disappointed with him. He shook his head a little sorrowfully as though he were dealing with an errant pupil he'd expected more from.

"Those are really misplaced values, man. These days you've got to get beyond that if you want to get anywhere.

A real artist lives by the blood. And blood is quarrelling, bitching, the bitch blood. I'm telling you. There's no art without domination. Impact. Like screwing. Hard and soft. That's where it begins, man. You have to face it."

"I suppose I just can't see it that way, that's all," said Walter, more meekly than he'd intended. But inwardly he was seething. When they reached the farm and he went upstairs, he found it painful even to roll down Rutner's sheets. Pompous egomaniac! What was he trying to do to her anyway? Rub her into the mud? The *cash* mattress! Was he some kind of con–artist all of a sudden?

He found it comforting to take Judy's side like this and imagined himself explaining Rutner's real nature to her, getting her to understand, exposing him once and for all. Rutner was barbaric, grasping, cruel. *He* at least was civilized! But instead of going to bed, Walter plunked himself down by the open window and gazed fixedly out over the apiary. The night air was cool, and the throb of crickets rode across it from the nearby fields. Near the stand of hollyhocks, fireflies had congregated, their bodies pulsing with that strange electric nectar, on–off, on–off, like Christmas lights. Still Walter couldn't relax. He would think of Rutner running his hand across Judy's breast, then making a lecture out of it, and he would ruminate even longer, pent up, vindictive, nursing his grievances. Why did he have to listen to all that? The 'func' sound. Like flunky. That had probably been meant for him too! Furious, he banged his fist down on the side of the old brown armchair until the dust flew. What was he *doing* here then? Especially when he could just pick up and clear out?

This thought pleased Walter enormously. He imagined the empty room the next morning, Rutner coming up the stairs, opening the door, the look of consternation on his face. And he himself off, out from under! What better way to show his defiance? All he needed to do was to wait for the creep to go to bed, give him time to get to sleep, then make his move. Leave him behind, like a bad idea.

Walter mulled over his plans through another pipe of tobacco, by the end of which he'd become slightly fogged by the smoke and impatient with the time. 10:20. And he'd heard the muffled clack of Rutner's typewriter for at least the last half hour. Helmut was composing. How long he'd be there was anybody's guess, and Walter began to wonder if he oughtn't just go down and confront him, tell him he had to go. He'd already stayed long enough, hadn't he? And yet he had a kind of nameless dread of Helmut Rutner, as though Helmut were somehow in a position to judge him, humiliate him, even. Walter felt suddenly stifled, uncertain. Maybe there was something to what Rutner said? It seemed to work, after all, however barbaric Walter considered it, and he found himself diffident, unable to confront Rutner on any solid ground even in his imagination.

No, it couldn't be. It was cruel, what Helmut proposed, sordid and cruel. How could he think otherwise? The crude, animal–man, like a shaggy billy–goat in the rutting season, mounting his she–goats with a slap on the haunches and a bitter, derisive laughter. How could he believe otherwise?

The thought occurred to Walter to put a good face on things and leave the next morning, but he couldn't stand the idea of getting between Rutner's sheets again. They were musty. They smelt odd, as though Rutner practised strange laundry habits. If he got between them he felt he would be trapped. Instead he crept out into the hallway near the stairs and looked over the railing. Underneath the study door on the first floor there issued a pale patch of light. He could still make out the faint tap of the typewriter, the silent sounds of alien concentration. Walter crept back to his room. Strange how his heart was beating!

Then at about eleven o'clock he made another *sortée* into the hallway. The patch of light under Rutner's study door was still there, but a long silence ensued. For five minutes Walter crouched near the railing, listening. Then a short, sharp ratchet roll of paper being torn from the carriage signalled another dismal span of Helmut's work. Walter snuck back into his room thinking perhaps his nerves might have given him away. Waiting so long in the chair by the window, planning his strategy had given him a nervous chill, but he was afraid to get up and pace around for fear it would really tip Rutner off.

Absurd! He knew what he was doing was absurd, and yet he couldn't stop. Instead he sat hunched up, squinting at his watch in the moonlight, trying to anticipate every detail of his escape. He imagined Rutner asleep, the house quiet, still. There was a door, for example, between the living room and the kitchen, a painted door with a black porcelain knob—almost certain to be shut. Now there was a major obstacle! Should he open it slowly, inch by inch or in one full motion? Walter spent the next few moments deliberating over this. What about Rutner's dog near the stove? Or the car starting?

It was another twenty minutes before he heard Helmut rummaging about in his own bedroom. Then, mercifully, the click of the light. He gave him another half hour to get to sleep. Finally, near midnight, Walter Taylor slipped into his jacket, took his pack, and made his way painfully down the stairs. How cold he was! Once or twice a tell–tale creak made him pause, and when he did he realized he was shivering. Best to stop completely and wait, he would think, and he repeated to himself what Rutner had told him to do when bees landed on his hands: freeze and wait for them to leave. He moved silently through the living room over the thin rug and negotiated the door, painstakingly, and he noted proudly (despite his beating heart) that he had done this with the kind of higher calm that came from doing a job purposefully and with enterprise. Was this how soldiers felt? He was heartened by the analogy.

The dog was nothing. A few thumps of her tail in recognition, and then, for no reason, the catastrophe. He heard the light in Rutner's room, heard the rustling of clothing, the inevitable footsteps, all with a panicked sense of bewilderment and, more surprising, of bitter, inexplicable amusement.

"Hey, what's up?"

Walter was momentarily blinded by the light. But he didn't have presence of mind enough to bluff. His face was too crimson to have pulled it off, Helmut too real standing there with his hairy legs, his slippers, and his dressing gown.

"Oh, nothing," Walter said as he walked out the screen door.

"Hey! Jesus! Where're you going?"

"Hey! Jesus! Where're you going?"

Walter could hear Helmut following behind him. He felt himself quickening his steps. Then he was running.

"Hey!" he heard again.

He reached the car seconds before Helmut and managed to lock the door. Blanched, stupid, Rutner's face stood framed by the car window. Walter wouldn't look at it.

"Look, Taylor, there's some real truth you don't want to face, you know. Something really basic."

Walter could feel the corners of his mouth turn down in contempt, an intensity of hatred well up in him. Still he wouldn't look at him. Though Helmut had his hand in the door handle, he switched on the ignition.

"You should take a look at yourself, Taylor. This sort of hostility is really unproductive. You know that."

Did he have to go on listening to these ravings? Did he have to put up with him? Slowly he stepped on the gas.

He heard the words, "*Jesus Christ!*" Helmut's hand was somehow caught in the door handle, and for a second or two Walter saw him running alongside the car as it headed down the driveway. But Walter wasn't about to stop. He pushed harder on the gas, swerving away from him as if to wrench himself free and clipping the gate post with his fender, just as Helmut let out an absurd cowboy yell.

"Aiee–yooo!"

Heart pounding, gravel pinging off the underside of his car, Walter Taylor made off down the road.

xiii

AT NINE–THIRTY the following morning Walter was standing in the hallway of Judy Stoddard's apartment. He had rung the bell. Now, frightened, but determined, he listened for the sound at the top of the stairs.

"Walter! What are you doing here!"

"Oh, nothing really," he said looking up the stairway and forcing a smile. "I thought you might like some help."

She seemed happy enough to see him. After he'd announced he hadn't eaten anything, she offered to make him breakfast, even though it meant shifting the newspapers in the kitchen out of the way. In the middle of the smell of gas cooking and fresh paint, Walter sank a little thankfully into a corner. He dug his hands deeper into his pockets and tried to relax. Rutner wasn't going to be there, he would tell himself. Rutner was correcting the proofs for *Rasputin*. He had the whole morning and at least part of the afternoon.

He had slept that night in a set of old apartments under renovation and he told Judy about these, the plaster

stripped to the lath, the intricacy of copper pipes connect-
ing one apartment to the next.

"I had the honour of sleeping beside a pile of sand,"
he added as he cupped his hands and held them up to the
light. "Streetlights, peace and quiet. I really recommend
it."

"Aren't you staying with Helmut any more?" Judy
suddenly asked him.

Walter was taken aback by the directness of the
question. He'd hoped to circle around this, get at it more
obliquely, but, "No," he replied, as blandly as he possibly
could. "Helmut and I had—Well, you might say we had a
falling out."

"Oh?"

"Yes. The kind of thing I was telling you about. He
can be awfully irritating."

Judy looked at him quizzically, and Walter twisted a
little in his seat.

"You know," he said, gathering up the pieces of the
speech he'd thought up the previous night, "I once knew
a fellow like Helmut. A red–haired man with only one leg.
He wanted to become a great artist. As a matter of fact, he
wanted it so badly he used to lock the doors to his readings
and not let anyone out. Not that too many people wanted
to leave. He had a fine voice. Captivating. But he was an
arriviste. His great obsession was making it. It was all he
talked about. And he seemed to know just how to go about
it. Television, film scripts, articles—everything."

Judy seemed interested as he spoke, and this encouraged him. What he disliked about all this, he said, (and he
made it clear in his own way how much he'd learned about

it staying with Helmut) was the insufferable egotism of such people. There were so many of them at it, a pack of ego–maniacs all jacking their heads up by pushing down on the next guy's. How he hated them! Their posters, their blab, their childish arguing. There was something of that in *Rasputin,* didn't she agree?

Judy was non–committal, and all Walter could do was retreat to a lame statement of his own. He wanted something less presumptuous, more modest, and he groped to articulate it as if it were the basis of a new–found creed.

"You know, this red–haired fellow got involved with the wife of a professor. They had farms near each other in Connecticut, and she started piling up Russian books between herself and her husband, right in the bed, and not letting him sleep with her. The usual turmoil. They seem to provoke it, people like that. They really want to destroy things."

Walter's eyes were by now moist with fellow–feeling and good intention, and he noticed as he talked that Judy herself had slowly nodded in approval and once or twice murmured, "I know," as though she did understand what he was saying and really valued these perceptions. He had touched her, then. A sense of quiet pleasure flooded over him, and he began to feel very warmly disposed towards her. Did it matter that he'd never really known such people and had only read about them in a book? Under the circumstances, it seemed the mildest of ruses. He told himself that in order to be worldly you had to practise. He decided not to make things hard on himself.

They painted that morning, went out for lunch, laughed together, and returned early in the afternoon. Walter made only one mistake. During a coffee break, in the middle of a bit of trivial conversation, he had taken her hand in his and Judy had taken it away again. Immediately he thought of the alternatives he'd plotted out for himself before he'd come over. If she doesn't come across, leave. No hanging around. No humiliating backtracking. No more of what had happened with Nathalie or with Rutner for that matter. That was how his new personality would deal with the problem. But he waited until they'd feigned starting to paint before trying again—and not without success. Windows open, his forearm still spattered, amid the faintly putrid scent of latex paint, Walter spent an afternoon coaxing her, saying silly things, convincing her how much more solid his approach was, how much more moral, and passing poisonous little remarks about Rutner with which she always seemed to agree.

"I think we have to sleep together," he finally said, as though he were proposing scaling a cliff.

"I'm not sure, Walter," she replied. "Don't you think it's a little soon?"

But she gave in in the end, and Walter could imagine no more wholesome relief to his chafed spirits than what transpired on her bedroom mattress for the rest of that afternoon and on into the early evening. In that one successful ray of sunshine that had managed to pierce an opening in the green sheet Judy had tacked over her bedroom window, Walter contemplated this victory, this peace and triumph. Four times. *Four times in a row!* Afterwards he would repeat this to all the assembled enemies of his imagination like a spell or an incantation. How could they ignore *four times in a row?*

And around eight, just as he and Judy were having some toast and instant coffee on the bedroom mattress, Helmut Rutner called on the telephone. Walter, who twigged, was almost beside himself with joy.

"Who was it?" he asked.

"Oh, Helmut, of course."

"Well, what did he want?"

"He wanted to come over," Judy said, smiling a little.

"So? What did you tell him?"

"I said I was busy."

"Busy!"

"Yes. He wanted to help me paint, but I told him I had some letters to write."

Walter chuckled. "So what did he say then?"

She shrugged. "He argued a bit. Then he hung up."

Three quarters of an hour later when he and Judy had just finished showering together and were eating more toast on the bedroom mattress, they heard a sharp knock at the door.

"Shh!"

Walter held his finger up to his lips and motioned Judy back to the mattress, and when she appeared to ignore him he said, "Shh!" again, waving impatiently at her, and tip–toed up to the door. Another sharp burst of knocking. He stooped a little, holding his breath, and looked through the peep–hole. Black. Pitch black. Puzzled, he squinted and looked again just in time to see the strands of the familiar beard retreating from the glass. The bastard had had his ear to the door!

"Come on, Judy," Rutner said. "It's me."

He knocked even more fiercely.

"Let me see," whispered Judy, coming over to him. She stood on her tip–toes and tried to look out, but another rain of blows made her jump back.

"*Judy!* For Christ's sake!"

Her mouth fell open. Walter's glee began to disappear. Judy looked toward the ceiling and pointed at her temple with her finger.

"Look, Judy! I know you're in there. I want to talk to you."

More knocks, then an unnatural pause. Judy looked at Walter apprehensively, but he just shook his head and squinted back into the hole. A small Pakistani woman had opened the door to her room and was staring out at the little drama. Then chortling, almost hysterical, Helmut's laughter rebounded off the door. Walter heard him fling off down the stairs. He raced to the living room window and peeped round the drapes just as a clot of earth and soft grass hit the pane.

xiv

THE FOLLOWING WEEKS, while Judy was away at the office, Walter would read or add to her record collection—judiciously; he was trying to educate her tastes. He'd discovered Bach and Telemann, and would regularly adjust his moods to fit in to what he considered their higher sense of harmony. Sometimes he was successful, though often it was with a cloying sense of dullness that he found curious coming from what was by all accounts great music.

He replaced Judy's cartoon posters, too. He would browse afternoons in bookshops, buying prints and reproductions of drawings, taking them home in their brown paper wrappings, and surprising her with these little additions to their *ambiance*. She, for her part, would rush home after work in a kind of highsummer excitement bearing her own offerings, things she thought Walter would like, pastries, a bottle of wine. Then they would spend a dark, robust evening in bed behind the green sheet that still hung in her bedroom window. And often, whenever his lips strayed across the small mouthful of hair on Judy's nipples, Walter would remember how Helmut had sucked there too, and how Helmut had been the first to tell him of this. Then he would tip her over on her hands and knees and make love to her with renewed vigour and a strange, abstract determination that bordered almost on violence.

During these same weeks, with a young man's intolerant enthusiasm, Walter had established himself his breakfast ritual: bacon, eggs, a touch of the baroque masters on the FM radio. Then the fine idle mornings while Judy was at work, long shafts of sunlight across oak floors, coffee, a string quartet in the background. Paradise, he would think to himself. A quiet, unassuming, civilized paradise, of the sort he'd promised her as he was wooing her away from Rutner. On weekends they would visit old furniture shops. Walter would take home a rocker or a small bureau and spend the long August mornings scraping down paint or burnishing up the bare wood with steel wool. This was the way he would work off the annoying squatter's feeling that sometimes overcame him. And it did give him a sense of renewal, as if inwardly he were making himself over as well, though it never did quite compensate for his not having a job. Judy worked; he lounged, as he would put it in his more self-critical moments. He paid his share of the rent, but his fifteen hundred dollars soon dwindled to twelve, then to less than a thousand. Judy talked vaguely about him going back to university.

In the evenings they would stroll aimlessly downtown or toward the campus to feed squirrels. Sometimes on these walks Walter would feel a comfortable sort of pride, such as he could believe husbands must feel, as though he knew all women through this one and could now claim rightful place. At other times he would come home depressed and irritable after looking into the faces of the women he passed in the street and searching for some kind of nameless recognition. And on occasions he would get it, or what passed for it, and he would fan out with a breezy preeniness like a summertime cock of the walk. This little excitement would last an hour or so, and as they strolled he would talk volubly to Judy about his plans. Then he would come home tired and dejected and fall on his bed in a black, inexplicable misery. What was it that was bothering him? He couldn't say. And in these moods he would take to listing off all the annoying habits he'd discovered in Judy over the weeks they'd been together. Why did she have to dust everything in sight, for example? With her ubiquitous dustcloth and the checkered kerchief tied over her hair, she would make her rounds every other evening or so, never ostentatiously enough to be a reproach as he sat deliberately absorbing himself in some book, but with a motherliness about her bric–à–brac that Walter concluded was the sure sign of some sort of limitation. After all, was the place some kind of museum?

Still, not without deciding he was being generous about it, Walter determined to overlook this, just as he forgave her the Agatha Christie novels she would devour in bed while a set of giant blue rollers sat in her hair. But he had a harder time accepting her twice a month weekend flights to Philadelphia. Her mother was seriously ill with a kidney disease that had ruined all her happiness at seeing her husband finally successful in his chosen arena (the United States), not to mention her happiness with her splendid house on the Main Line, new furniture, and the fact that she'd finally left Winnipeg which she'd always hated.

"Why do you always go?" Walter had once asked.

"Because I think my mother needs me," Judy had answered.

But that was a mistake, Walter concluded in his paranoia. It wasn't that her mother wanted her home. Not really. He'd seen Judy's father only in the military photographs she kept by her bed: Geoffrey Stoddard, age twenty–six in his army beret and his vacuum–cleaner salesman smile and his intolerable hypocrisy. Even from the photos Walter had visions of him whoring and drinking his way through the war. He *knew* this was what had happened, and he guaranteed himself, just by intuition, that her father was the moving spirit behind those Thursday night phonecalls which Judy both dreaded and adored and to which she responded by cursing the Americans, cursing Geoffrey's manipulation, and automatically packing her valise. *He* wanted his daughter around in these moments of crisis, and Judy never said no. It irked Walter, particularly since she wouldn't breathe a word of his existence for fear of upsetting her mother. He had to languish for his pains in the shades of non–entity, and he decided, since Geoffrey Stoddard was to blame for this, he would detest him as much as he pleased.

On the whole he would have said he liked living with Judy. He liked the gloomy, muscular residence she lived in, dark from too much stained glass window dressing and shaded by horse chestnut trees. He liked the freedom it gave him. He liked the walks he would take to a small coffee–house in Yorkville where in midafternoons he would order Hungarian pastries and café mocha, light up his pipe, and listen for an hour or two to the accents of the Eastern European customers. Often at times his thoughts would stray to Nathalie Doroshkov, and he would tuck his book unread into his back pocket and walk home again, scanning the faces of the passing women, this time for some resemblance of her, and when he found one, as he sometimes did, he would arrive home cold and irritable and withdraw from Judy in subtle ways for the rest of the evening.

He had told Judy little of Nathalie, and what little he did only made a satisfying mystery out of his relationship with her. And sometimes as he sat idly in the café on August weekday afternoons, he would muse over her name, imagining her hard, taut boyish limbs, trained and graceful, and the echo of the pinpricks of pleasure would suffuse his body, only distantly now, without the intensity of those few weeks back, and he would feel strangely saddened by the memory of her liveliness and vivacity. Once when Judy was away, he'd parked outside Kusiuski's house until two o'clock in the morning, watching the shadows in the windows and keeping an eye on the front door to see who might come and go until he was bored to a stupor.

Nor did he and Judy discuss Helmut Rutner any more, because as far as Walter was concerned, he was contemptible, part of a dead past. And yet often on these afternoon vigils of his, something in the sight of a passing figure would remind him of Helmut, and a sudden escalator of fear would descend inexplicably from the pit of his stomach to the back of his knees. Then he knew he dreaded meeting him again, and because he couldn't say why he felt ashamed.

Of course, there were minor inconveniences, too, like the fact that Judy wouldn't let him answer the phone between eight–thirty and nine in the morning. That was when her boss, Miss Dorset, sometimes called with last minute instructions, and Miss Dorset wouldn't have approved of her junior staff living with young men. Nothing irritated Walter more than this little interdiction, but whenever he suggested where Miss Dorset could go, Judy would tell him that jobs weren't easy to come by.

Visits from relatives posed problems too. Judy didn't want her parents to know she was living with her boyfriend. Neither did her best friend, Judy would say when Walter got mad—and later she'd apparently gone to the length of promising to install a lock on the bedroom door of her apartment so she could prove to her mother that she really did have a separate room. Worse, when Judy's uncle Randolph and his wife Jane came in from Hamilton to discuss her mother's illness, Judy fell into a quandary about what to do with Walter's things.

"Do you think they would fit in the cupboard?" she asked.

"Why? They're not going to see anything."

"Of course they'll see, Walter." Then she looked at him. "And what about you? Couldn't you go out for a walk or something?"

"A walk? Where?"

"Well, you *can't* be here, Walter. Please don't make things difficult for me."

Walter finally decided he'd hide in the cupboard too. His junk was piled up behind him, and Judy's dresses kept swinging in his face. He didn't dare sit down for fear something might topple. Besides he wanted to keep his ear to the door. But he had no idea how stiflingly hot a cupboard could become, and when Aunt Jane kept Judy talking for at least a half an hour he would say to himself, "Hurry up, Jesus!" as the sweat dampened the hair on his temples.

Worst of all, perhaps, was Judy's telling him that Rutner had come over one evening that week when he'd been out. This was more than Walter could bear.

"What did he want?" he asked testily. "Did he come in and snoop around?"

"Not really. I gave him some ice cream and showed him the chair you were working on."

Walter screwed up his face.

"Bastard," he muttered as he paced around the floor. "He probably came to spy. Did he ask you anything?"

"No. He was quite stiff, really. I don't know why you're getting so upset."

"Because he's prying, that's why. He just wants to come in here with his harebrained notions and make judgements. It's like an invasion. He comes in, looks over your life, carries it off, then picks it apart, the creep."

"Oh, Walter. I think you're just exaggerating."

"No, I'm not exaggerating. We'll see if I'm exaggerating."

He paced around a bit more, then turned toward her. "Did you invite him here, by any chance?"

"Walter!"

"I'm asking. Did you invite him?"

"Walter, I did *not* invite him. He doesn't mean anything to me. Really he doesn't. I don't know how you could ask such a thing."

"I can ask, don't worry. I know that bastard like the back of my hand. Weasling around. He's a shit, o.k.? A pile of shit!"

XV

TWO WEEKS LATER, one afternoon in mid–September, Judy had gone off again to Philadelphia, leaving Walter with the weekend to kill. He'd taken his coffee cup over to the window and was staring outside. The occasional fan–shaped span of horse chestnut leaves had already turned yellow. It was damp and unseasonably cold, and yet he noticed a few more people out on the sidewalks than usual. Shopping, of course. It was Saturday. Walter's thoughts turned for a moment to Judy. She would have landed by now, her father having lured her back, successful to the end. There would be thick steaks on the outdoor barbeque. There would be the usual sniping and bickering over business or American foreign policy. Her brother would be playing touch football; her mother would be less seriously ill than her father had implied, and Judy would feel used and duped all weekend long and return vowing never to cross the border again. It had happened before. It was one of her favourite topics of conversation. In her perky, cynical manner she enjoyed discussing her differences with her father, his blundering summonses, his guilt–mongering. There *had* been the re-lapse, she would remind Walter whenever he became too incredulous, only her father milked it for all it was worth.

And now this was the fourth weekend she had flown down since he'd moved in, the story always the same: mother was coping, very well whenever *he* wasn't around with his third–base coach approach to illness. Geoffrey Stoddard, nursemaid, who'd had an exercycle installed in the bedroom, and who would help his wife out of bed every morning and make her ride it. "Not to overdo it, chicken," he would say to Judy when she asked about this by way of protest. "But I *don't* want your mother an invalid, do you understand?"

Of course, Walter would remind himself, Judy could never be sure her father's telephone manner of martini–stoked, formal frenzy mightn't be a signal for genuine concern. Life Geoffrey Stoddard had learned to meet with a pervasive sense of high crisis, a carry–over from French war days both splendid and horrible when he'd cleared out his share of Nazis from the local rubble heaps. This was Judy's explanation. Nightmare month was June, it seemed, and it continued to be for the rest of his life, yet, according to her, he looked back on his memories with a mixture of passion and regret and tried to defend himself against his daughter's charges whenever she forced him to. Above all he wanted to preserve his martyrdom. He'd sent her to a lily–white university run by a farmteam from the Oxford group, though he'd thought his native Canadians would have had more sense. Besides, degrees didn't help you understand fourth quarter pressure anyway. "You won," he would say to her with some contempt, during their disputes about American involvement in Viet Nam. "You won, or you got it in the ass."

Walter put on the record of his string quartet again, passively enduring the first two movements to get to the only part he liked, but even that didn't work. He paced around nervously. Then he tossed his jacket on and walked past the university. The students had all returned, filling up bookstores and fast food joints, parties of girls and young men, laughing and talking. Walter felt a tug of nostalgia for not being one of them. Then he dropped down into the campus itself and wasted an hour on a park bench. Young women passed him by, and he would look up into their faces as though he could read their minds. Bored, irritable, he finally wandered over to his café, bought a paper and a package of dry Dutch cigars, the kind Helmut Rutner used to smoke, and sat down. And after reading, after smoking and musing, he rose with a slight smile on his face and left. It took him only a twenty minute walk through the downtown crowds to reach the ballet studio.

Up the stairs, through the passageway with the grey signs, a turn to the left, and there on that cloud–darkened afternoon, a children's class was dancing, small girls with braids, with pony–tails, unformed, their hesitant landings and turnings filled with curious certainty. Yet so quick to laugh and giggle they were, so nonchalant about the serious business of dance! Some mothers had gathered near the doorway, and Walter found himself among them, trying to piece parent and daughter together as best he could. Strange how a face was altered down the long corridor of the generations, he would think, mothers knitted with fathers together, resemblances at times acute, at times reduced to traces, a look, an inflexion of the body. These were the parsings of the flesh, and for a moment, as small girls raised their legs imperfectly to a prelude by Chopin, Walter felt he understood that pride and expectancy written in their mothers' faces. Resurrection, she had said. Resurrection! Dimly, in the back of his mind he wondered if that was what Judy's mother had expected for her daughter too.

Down the corridor still, rhythmic, muscular, the music of Bach, the mallet–tap of toe–shoes across a bare floor. An aging ballerina, overweight, yet surprisingly swift, sure, led a foursome in *pas de cheval.* Minus the sunlight on this lengthening afternoon, their exertions seemed little more than human, just this struggle to overcome the larger inertia of things, the strain, the flicker of frustration at a wobbly landing, the eternal specific gravity of limitation. There was an edge to the ballet mistress' voice as she rapped her stick smartly on the floor to emphasize a point. And when from the corner of the room Nathalie's eyes met his, Walter felt the sudden rush of fear mixed with excitement descend through his limbs. What would he say to her? Had she even recognized him? He wondered if he had broken her concentration and distracted her.

"Walter!" she cried when she had finally finished, flushed and sweating, out of breath, and was undoing the pink ribbons on her shoes. "I thought you were out west!"

"No," he said. "This is as far as I got."

"But why? I mean you seemed so *prepared*. All those apples you had in your car, maps...."

"Oh," he said, looking sheepish. "I suppose you could say I got waylaid."

"Oh, Walter. Come *on*, now. I'm sure you have all *sorts* of adventures to tell me about. Where are you staying."

"Oh," he said vaguely. "I've got a place on Walmer Road."

"That's wonderful, Walter!"

She invited him for coffee, the same cakeshop where they made the best mocha squares. What had he been doing with himself? Did he have a girlfriend? She was sure he had a girlfriend. She peppered him with gay little questions, hardly giving him a chance to answer, a small mercy for which he inwardly thanked her, and he continued to beam ambiguously and leave things tantalizingly open. It occurred to him he might even ask her back to the apartment, until he imagined her opening Judy's cupboard door. How would he explain? He lived with a cousin he hadn't thought it important to mention? He felt even more nervous and dug his hands even deeper into his pockets.

"And what about you?"

He was trying to be solicitous. Best to be solicitous, he told himself.

"Oh, well, Walter," she said breezily. "Life goes on, you know. We all have our stories to tell."

He hesitated a moment. They had reached the shop, and he stopped to open the door. "You sound as though you really have one," he said as she led the way down the aisle.

"Do I?"

"Well...."

He shrugged.

"A lot happens when you go to another city. Really a lot. And Helmut's been a real saviour to me. If he hadn't known where I could go, I don't know what I would have done."

"This was in New York?"

"Oh, yes. Darling New York."

As she spoke, Walter pursed his lips. He was determined to be stoical.

"I can't stay in one place, you know Walter," she said, almost divining his thoughts. "I'm just not built like that."

"No, of course."

"Anyway, I got pregnant."

Walter looked up at her.

"Yes. But it's alright now. I got an abortion."

"Just like that?"

"What did you want me to do? Have this *rat* growing in me?"

He was puzzled. He had never seen her quite so worked up as this.

"Believe me, Walter, that's what it was. This creep of creeps I met in New York. I won't tell you how it happened. It's too disgusting. Here, do you want something?"

Nathalie handed him the menu, but he decided to let her order.

"Anyway...." she said.

There was a silence. Then he looked up at her again. He felt immensely, ridiculously betrayed, but it was a betrayal that stayed remote from him, as if in some other corner of his body, leaving him free to be as serene as he liked. It was almost as though he felt comfortable with these revelations, as though they were on common ground.

"So what happened?" he finally asked.

"Oh—" She breathed a short contemptuous breath. "Walter, you can't imagine what a despicable New York creep I had on my hands. It makes me sick to think about it. You know how some people are mad about Slavic women. Just *mad* about them. The Slavic soul thing—which I don't believe in, by the way. Well, he would come to my door and cry, literally cry unless I let him in. And he was so rich I said why not? If you want to throw your money around. He was a stock market analyst. Money coming out of his ears. And do you know he would promise me an eighteen room chateau? He lived in an absolute dump himself, but he was going to buy an eighteen room chateau! Ha ha ha!"

Walter gave her a wan smile.

"Well, it was a complete fluke, you know. First I had my period. Second he promised he wouldn't come inside, but of course he did, and.... Do you realize that was the second time in a week that happened to me? First you, Walter, and then—I mean, *really.* I've had nightmares for the past month. I would dream of the thing with an i.u.d. sticking out of its head, and I wasn't even wearing one, for god's sake!"

Something about what she was saying made Walter inexpressibly angry. And yet, curiously, as she told him her story she had never been more attractive to him, and he felt his underpinnings rot and loosen, and he began to feel lost.

"If it was so terrible, what did you get mixed up with him for?" he finally asked, harshly. Nathalie's face grew blank, and she seemed to reach back into herself to call on a rich inner source of self–justification.

"I don't think you understand I was trying to commit suicide," she said. "I was very upset at the time."

"What do you mean?"

"I mean I was depressed, terribly depressed. I wanted to die. And as he was doing it, I imagined he was a great bug crawling all over me, a black spider or something. I didn't care what happened to me, don't you understand that? Of course, god punished me—I never imagined for a moment.... Do you know in my dreams I could see this replica of him growing inside me? His head was indented at the temples—some problem at birth, and his eyes were buggy." She shuddered. "Oh, nature is vile, detestable. I hate it. All of sex, so filthy and disgusting. And it's all men think about, can you imagine? Really, do you want to know what my dream is? Just to go to Paris and study with Carmena Ouspenskaia, pliés and arabesques all day long. Don't you think that would be divine?"

Walter sat tongue–tied, toying with his coffee spoon, staring at the froth he made with his whipped cream. Café à la viennois, café mocha, he would read to himself on the menu, and the thought of the small girls at their ballet class came to him, the ones with the braids and the pony–tails, and he would imagine himself crossing the continent together with Nathalie, the night train to Brussels, Dussel-dorf, Mainz, Berlin, an expensive meal in the darkness, afterwards a little dry Dutch cigar. A faint reminiscent rush of the pinpricks of pleasure descended slowly through his stomach to his knees.

"Walter, are you *listening* to me?"

"Yes, of course."

"You're not going to light that thing up in here, are you?"

"Why not?"

"Because it stinks, that's why. I know why all you men smoke those things anyway."

"No you don't."

"God, look at you holding your thumb in your hand, for heaven's sake!"

He stopped hiding his thumb.

"Now Walter," she said. "What's the matter?"

"What?"

"I know there's something the matter, so you might as well tell me. Is it the story I just told you?"

"Not a terribly nice story...."

"I thought so. Now listen, Walter," she began.

But something was bothering him and he had to interrupt her.

"No. Wait. Please! Just tell me one thing. I— Look, do you mind if I ask you? Are you sure it was his child?"

"Whose?"

"The fellow in New York."

She paused in a moment of uncertainty, and then it dawned on her.

"Walter!" She looked at him with her eyes widened. "You can't believe—" Then she burst out laughing. "Ha! ha! ha! Do you really think? Oh, that's priceless."

"What's so funny?"

"I don't know. It just is."

"But don't you think— I mean, if you had had the child you wouldn't have known who the father was."

"So?"

"Don't you think that makes a difference?"

Two kinds of sperm, he would think to himself, two colours of plasticine kneaded together, his nose, a New York leg. She could pick and choose.

"Oh, Walter, don't preach," she began.

She was going to lecture him, he thought. She was going to tell him he had no right to sit there like a morbid judge, feeling injured about what was a perfectly normal, even banal experience, something he had better learn about instead of casting his silly hurt aspersions and acting like a sulky schoolboy. Of course she was right. She was going to tell him. And yet even as he was preparing to listen to this, he realized that that wasn't what she'd had in mind. There was no lecture. He might have been more grateful if there had been. Instead she was only telling him how she had to leave, how she was sorry he didn't understand, how perhaps one day he would.

"I've really got to go now," she said, motioning to get up. "You've no idea how tired I am."

"Hold on! Wait," Walter said looking up at her, perplexed. "Finish your coffee at least." And after a moment's silence, he asked, "Don't you ever worry about being alone?"

"Alone!"

"Yes. I mean—"

"Oh, Walter, don't be so sentimental. Now, come on, shake hands."

"Shake hands? What for?"

"Because we're good friends. Now give me your hand, Walter."

Walter didn't want to give her his hand. He held back a moment, unsure of what to say to detain her, and then he resigned himself. Face averted, lips set, he shook hands, the same thin, almost ethereal handshake he remembered when he first met her. And after she left, disgruntled, wishing he'd said more, he walked slowly back to the apartment.

Why had he let her leave like that? Why couldn't he at least explain what he meant? He kicked a stone off the sidewalk into the metal grating in the road. And she was the one who wanted people to be like angels! *I am the resurrection and the life. Ballet is the resurrection and the life!* Walter swore to himself. What did she have to spoil things for? Why had she gone and messed everything up? He wound up to kick another stone when somewhere in the back of his mind it occurred to him it was Judy Stoddard's apartment he was going back to. He didn't care. He didn't care what he'd done. It made him all the angrier. The stone struck cleanly off the end of his shoe and dented the underside of a parked car. Two passersby looked at him askance.

When he got back, he flung himself across the bed in Judy's room. Almost in tears, he studied the photograph on her night–table. Geoffrey Stoddard's military beret looked out at him, brisk, clean, his smile irritating. For some inexplicable reason, his thoughts turned to Helmut Rutner, the absurd cowboy yell the night Walter had left him, the hysterical, derisive laughter, that passage from *Rasputin* Walter had pondered over with such morbid fascination. Then, in a moment of inspiration, he found a pair of scissors and flipped through Judy's encyclopedia,

until he came to a section on pigs that he'd once discovered. There were sixteen plates, of various species, sows
and boars. Of these he chose the boar with the most
unnaturally massive member, a huge old tuskless barn-
yard boarder with a tool the size of a roast, cut it out,
inserted it in the small gold frame, and placed it on the
night–table beside the bed like a little jewel.

xvi

THE NEXT MORNING, when Walter woke up, Judy was there, tip–toeing about, cleaning up.

"What are *you* doing home ?" he asked, after he'd got dressed and come out of the bedroom.

Judy smiled at him a little crookedly, unsure of his tone, and took some plates away into the kitchen.

"Oh, it was just as you'd said. Mother didn't seem so badly off, so I thought I'd leave her and Dad alone."

Walter nodded mutely and went and sat down on the couch. Judy seemed to feel some need to explain.

"I only spent yesterday with them, really. I was at the airport last night." Then, after a pause, "You don't seem too happy this morning."

"Oh, don't mind me. I'm just tired."

He knew she had come home early for his sake, but in his sullenness, he made no attempt to acknowledge it. For a moment Judy went back to her dusting.

"So how was your day?" she finally asked.

Morose, pre–occupied, Walter didn't answer.

"Walter?"

"Oh, o.k. I guess."

She looked at him, hurt. She turned to go back to her work once again, then pulled up short, went into the bedroom, and came back with the little gold–framed photograph he'd put there the day before.

"Walter, can you tell me what this is?"

"That? Oh. Nothing, really. Forget it. Just a little joke."

"Nothing? It doesn't seem like nothing to me. I don't find it very funny. It's awfully ugly, Walter."

"I suppose it is, isn't it," he said.

Judy wasn't quite sure how to take this. Then she turned to him, slowly, her dustcloth in her hands.

"I'm sorry, Walter, but I have something to show you."

She went to the hall to her travelbag and returned with a letter in a large brown envelope.

"I don't know why I packed it with my things when I left—I guess in the rush, but I'm afraid I opened it and read it."

Walter Taylor took the envelope from her hand. When he saw the characteristic miniscule black ink writing on the cover, his stomach sank. It was from Helmut Rutner. His hands trembled as he slipped out the letter.

Taylor!

FRIENDSHIP IS OPPOSITION.
Even though you're holed up in your bastion like an old numismatist of domesticity, I figured I would hold out the mythic olive branch, only with leaves dipped in herbal tea. The bourgeois disease (poetsbane) is insidious enough to attack all strong constitutions. (Symptoms: worry about

matching furniture, gardening, pretensions to gourman-dism.) Having escaped, I order prayers and thanksgiving to all nine muses and ask, "Would Nietzsche have gone back to his aunts?" For the bourgeois nesting instinct I recommend no spearmint placebos, but a boggling dose of the deities of the depths. Leading the pack: Dionysus, the life–in–death— the only sure–fire remedy.

I'm worried about your psyche, man. My own cure means just this, that real fertility is shrouded in the exhalations of death, though that doesn't help you. So watch it. Plunge into the soup of the irrational or your dancing spirit will dry up. Johnny Sartre said it. Watch possessions or they'll grab you like a cobra.

But don't get me wrong. As you know I'm not against women. I believe in whatever makes me darkly self–centered, exultant, whatever takes me back to my pristine baby state. That's the core of my creative genius, the Rasputin enthusi-asm, mesmeric, archetypes flowing through the veins, every contradiction under the sun.

You've got to stay away from the goddesses and the doormats, like Picasso says. The pendulum life: sheer hell. You have to find the true third way, preuxorian Eve I call her, civilization's foreskin. Item: buttery ass, ripe jumpy breasts, wine red hair, all fat and sass. That's my Melfi, man, my new bawd, once a whore in the Northwest Territories, the whole bloody wilderness up her tail like a mink in heat! That's my Melfi, fucking little Lilith,* resurrected. Jesus, I love her! Get ready for La Vita Nuova!

p.s. I never hold what a woman's done against her.

Helmut

* Lilith (in case you're interested): first wife of Adam, made by God from mud and filth, spawner of monsters.

p.p.s. Nathalie's beautiful, man. God damned beautiful!

Walter sat down. "Only a turd like Rutner would footnote his own letters," he muttered to himself. "Egomaniac."

"When did you get this?" he asked suspiciously.

"Friday afternoon. It was here, and I just packed it by mistake."

"*Jesus!*"

Walter got up and paced about the room. Then he took the letter from the side of the armchair, went into the bedroom and re–read it by the night–table where the picture had stood. An olive branch! He tried hard to stay calm. When all Rutner was doing was bullying and insulting with that face of his that had pigheadedness written all over it. Like a Prussian sausage. He sat down for a minute, then took the letter out a third time and read it over again. So he was Dionysus! Walter could hear him jibing at his life, laughing over him with his friends, and he suddenly felt empty and confused. Why did Judy have to let him in in the first place, the brazen crap–artist! He brought his fist suddenly down on the side of the armchair so that the dust flew up. "*Damn!* " he said, as he got up and walked back into the living room.

"Walter! What's the matter?"

"That's what comes of giving those bastards ice–cream!" he yelled. "What in hell did you have to let him in for?"

"Walter, I don't know what you're talking about!"

"Oh? This is what I'm talking about," and he slammed the open door back into the doorway with all the force he could muster.

"Walter! For god's sake!"

Then he walked over to the wooden rocking chair he was working on, raised it over his head, and brought it hurtling down against the floor. It smashed in three pieces. One jagged dowel, rocker attached, ricocheted off the dining room table.

"Walter! Have you gone crazy?"

He grabbed his keys off the table and went downstairs to his car.

All the way up north Walter had visions of Helmut Rutner in bed with his girlfriend, a fat, stupid girl with big tits, in every conceivable position. They would flip through his mind like pornographic stills, and when he tried to shake them away, she would be replaced first by Judy, then by Nathalie, and he would imagine them in the same position again, moaning and digging their fingernails into Rutner's flesh, while he himself looked on, passive, fascinated, and the empty confused feeling again overtook him. The bastard! The sleazy, pig–faced, conniving bastard! He knew what Rutner's Lilith would be like. He could just imagine her, long pioneer skirt, frizzy red hair, her fat feet ringed with dirt, the farmhouse awash with mugs and ashtrays and little nubs of dogfood that had rolled across the floor under the chairs. There would be a little pair of panties soaking in the sink.

Then Walter would imagine himself and Rutner together in the kitchen, alone. Walter would be stalking him, circling around him, waiting for his opportunity. Finally it would come. A left to the solar plexus, right cross to the jaw, all in slow motion, and Rutner would be on his knees in pain, his face screwed up, contrite, begging forgiveness, admitting everything. Or it was after a quick feint, a sudden wheeling motion, and then a stubborn little hammerlock, and Walter would be there behind him, inching his arm slowly past the shoulder blade, his mouth just next to Rutner's ear. It gave him enormous pleasure to imagine Rutner defeated in this way. It would make up for everything he'd done, all the sordidness he'd inflicted on everyone, on Judy, on Nathalie. If only he could bc defeated! Then he could be set aside, dealt with, for he'd become like a demon to Walter, an obsession, from which he *had* to be free. "*Lilith!*" Walter would say to himself in contempt, and he could feel the rage surge up in him again.

There was no one around when he arrived. Walter stopped in front of the farmhouse and wondered whether he ought to park in the driveway, considering what had happened the last time. "Do it," he finally ordered himself. "Do it, or shut up!"

He drove right up beside the house. As he knocked at the screen door, he heard some rustling inside; then suddenly the careful words he'd prepared in advance seemed to fly out of his head. What would he say? How would he explain himself?

The dog was shooed away. A figure was opening the door. But it was not what he had expected. Whoever she was, Lilith, Rutner's cousin, she was neat, trim, fair, with a spiritual, almost other–worldly quality to her as she gazed out at him. When she tilted her head back, quizzically, the tendrils of her hair seemed to curve about her long neck, soft, slightly curving, like a pillar of flesh. Walter, made awkward by her beauty, mumbled something, uncertain of his judgments now, bewildered in some recess of himself he couldn't name, and when he inquired, he was told Rutner was in the orchard. Slowly, hesitantly, Walter turned and retraced the familiar path.

Helmut was in his white suit when Walter first spotted him, the bee–veil he used partially obscuring his face as he leaned over a hive, then extracted a frame from the box and held it aloft toward the sun, suspended overhead.

"Should I call out to him now?" Walter wondered. "No," he thought, "Best to wait till he was finished."

Walter stood motionless in the grass some yards from the hives, Rutner's back towards him, the grass green, dark, intensely alive even in mid–September, the leaves of the elms behind touched with yellow. Rutner, in his veil and white suit, seemed like some confectionery spirit to preside over them all. Bees swooped crazily about, angry because it was cool, because it was mid–day, because it was almost autumn and they were jealous for their honey. Then, as he picked out a second frame, Rutner slowly turned.

"Hello, Walter," he said.

Bastard! He'd seen him all the time!

"I got your letter," Walter finally declared.

Helmut nodded.

"I think we should have it out."

"What's that?"

Walter raised his voice.

"I said I think we should have it out."

But Rutner paid no attention. He was absorbed by the heavy frame he held, his harvest, fat, rich, each octagonal cell stamped by its own brown granular cap and where a few drops of liquid trickled down from the bottom, bees in strings attached themselves, drunken, enraged.

"Hold on a moment, man. I'll be with you in a second."

Then Helmut replaced the hive cover and ambled slowly over.

"Well," he said, smiling affably. "What's up?"

Bullshit–artist. Walter looked him straight in the eye.

"I said I think we should have it out. I mean physically."

Physically! Did he have to talk that way? But Rutner was a boob. You had to dot all the i's. And yet Helmut seemed genuinely startled by this. As he took off his veil, a look of sudden disdain crossed his face.

"Look, I don't want to fight you, Walter," he said at last.

Walter felt the same intensity of hatred well up in him as it had that night at the farm. How to get him to understand? How to get through to this idiot how perverse he really was?

"Then you are a *coward!* "

Walter Taylor fairly spat out the words, but as he heard this nineteenth–century cliché pass his lips, he couldn't help feeling ridiculous. Rutner paused for a moment.

"So where do you want to do this?" he said, slightly bemused.

"In the field by the road. That'll be just fine."

For two or three minutes they circled around, fists raised, with no more than a few exploratory jabs to show

"For two or three minutes they circled around, fists raised...."

for their trouble. Walter was nervous, extremely nervous. He was cutting the air. Really he didn't want to hit him, was that it? He didn't really want to hit him. It took him the first few minutes to realize he was leading with his right.

But after the first blows landed, he dropped his illusions of uppercuts and smart right crosses. They would just rush at each other with flurries of wild punches that left him dazed and hurt. They would break, then a fist would find its way home and another shapeless torrent would begin, and he could feel his lip swell and his stomach knot in anticipation. Then once again he would find himself lashing out wildly, bringing his knuckles down on whatever he could reach, shoulders, the side of Rutner's head. He was gasping for breath.

Once from long range his fist found the mark on Rutner's face. There was a sickening popping sound. His knuckles stung from the blow. Then Rutner came at him, swearing under his breath, "Fucking little hypocrite!" and Walter felt himself backpedalling in exhaustion, taking a mess of punches to the side of the head, across the forehead, the bridge of his nose. Then as they broke, he found himself turning away, sinking to his knees, and suddenly he was sprawling on the grass. From the corner of his eye he could see Rutner walking away, the sunlight between the two yellowing elms glancing off his shoulders, stray bees, still angry, swooping in long arcs above his head.

How did he have the energy? Where did he get the energy? Walter himself had collapsed face–forward into the stubble of the field, and he was almost glad to be there. Slowly he felt himself sinking, losing himself almost thankfully in a daze, merging momentarily with the cool ground underneath. He could feel the bits of straw lodge in his hair as he lay, and in what seemed almost an eternity, an ant began to crawl from the earth up over the side of his cheek. Then the perspiration and the waves of nausea overcame him, and he felt as though he were scouring up the last dregs of his body. Not vomit. Never vomit, but an inky, glaucous bile, slick, stinking, green as the grass it sat on. And after a quarter of an hour, once he'd staggered into his car, he retched another pool on the floor near the front seat.